A Peace In Time

First Edition Design Publishing

A Peace In Time
Copyright ©2014 Herschel Waller

ISBN 978-1622-876-32-7 PRINT
ISBN 978-1622-876-33-4 EBOOK

LCCN 2014941186

May 2014

Published and Distributed by
First Edition Design Publishing, Inc.
P.O. Box 20217, Sarasota, FL 34276-3217
www.firsteditiondesignpublishing.com

ALL RIGHTS RESERVED. No part of this book publication may be reproduced, stored in a retrieval system, or transmitted in any form or by any means — electronic, mechanical, photo-copy, recording, or any other — except brief quotation in reviews, without the prior permission of the author or publisher.

To
Nancy,
the love of my life,
and
to
the long-forgotten Sarah

To every thing there is a season, and a time to every purpose under heaven...

Ecclesiastes 3:1

A Peace In Time

by
Herschel Waller

Chapter One

Sarah Bollinger, dead at only eighteen years of age, was laid to rest in the cold mud. A chilling light rain fell through the longleaf pine branches as the pallbearers removed the unadorned wooden casket from an ebony-colored wagon. The weeping women in dark gowns and bonnets and the stern men in ashen cloaks staring across the cemetery toward the plantation house created a tableau in black and gray. Normally filled with laughter, the house sat silent now, its eaves dripping with tears from heaven, its vitality sapped by the tragedy of Sarah's death.

"Ashes to ashes, dust to dust..." the minister recited monotonically as the coffin was lowered into the blackness of the deep, loamy hole.

The slaves watched in a small group from afar, some of them wiping their eyes with worn, leathery hands. Finally, the plaintive strains of an old prayer rose through the drooping tree branches toward the leaden sky, and it was over.

*****

Overheated by the blazing East Texas sun, Granger Walker used the sleeve of his shirt to wipe the sweat pouring off his freckled forehead. Though he and his wife Teresa were accustomed to the heat, this summer of 2005 had been particularly brutal. The broken cement sidewalks around them generated waves of blasting heat like steaming griddles on a hot stove, and even the tall pines seemed to shrivel in the swelter.

"Over here. I think it's this way, but it's been a while since I was here last," he called to Teresa as he squinted in search of his great-grandfather's grave. Using his height to advantage, he peered over the tops of a row of cedar bushes in the direction of a distant magnolia tree.

Granger had visited Balfour Cemetery many times during his youth. The neat rectangular plots were almost all occupied now, most having been filled during the nineteenth and early twentieth century. The tilted and fractured monuments reflected an earlier time, when miniature Parthenons and oversized lamenting angels embellished the final resting places of the affluent and simple gray slabs marked the graves of those of more modest means. Here Granger had learned about death as well as life; here he had absorbed family culture and traditions. He was rooted in this place.

"Oh, I found it." He waved at Teresa across five rows of monuments as he read the marker that rose only about two feet out of the clay-laced topsoil.

Francis Granger Lee
September 24, 1867
August 13, 1939

"Wow, the stone's a lot smaller than I remember. Guess things just look bigger when you're a kid."

"Okay, you found it. Let's go," Teresa blurted out as she adjusted her heavily tinted sunglasses and pressed a handkerchief against her tanned cheek. She felt the dampness in her dark curly hair and craned her neck toward the sound of her husband's voice. Despite standing on her toes, she couldn't see over the cedars. "Granger, where are you going? Hurry up. You'll blister in this sun." Then, after a moment, "*Granger*! It's too hot to be out here." Her voice trailed off as she realized his attentions were elsewhere. Desperate for shade, she leaned up against a towering pine tree and rolled up her sleeves as far as she could.

In the distance, Granger was rattling on. "I was named after him, you know. He was a merchant here in Balfour for a long time. He married late in life...."

Teresa was thinking about the cool air conditioning back at the house and about where they might have dinner later. As she pondered the question of food and Granger rambled about his family tree, she noticed an old slab lying barely above ground level nearby. The badly cracked gray marble lay horizontally atop crumbling bricks walling the sides of the grave. She strained her eyes and lifted her sunglasses to read the barely legible words.

Sarah Ellen Bollinger
Aged 18 Years, 6 Months and 20 Days
Died January 9, 1855

It was simple but poignant. Suddenly, her eyes welled with tears. Granger and Teresa's daughter Victoria would have been eighteen now, a young woman, perhaps with her mother's olive skin and her father's flashing blue eyes. She would surely have been both intelligent and beautiful, the desire of all the boys and the delight of her parents. They had lost their only chance for immortality so long ago. Teresa was still hurting, and the pain was even greater because the accident that took her life didn't seem to bother Granger any more.

She turned her attention back to the stone at her feet, and, inexplicably, she felt compelled to run her fingers along the indentations of the inscription. In an instant Teresa was overcome, her head reeled, and she thought she was about to faint. She felt a wave of empathy, a stark understanding of the somber ceremony in the cold rain so many years ago.

*****

"Come, Mother, we have to go." Robert's hand gently pulled at her shawl-covered shoulder.

"No…no, I can't leave her here. She needs me." Vivian sobbed almost silently and touched a lace handkerchief to her eyes.

"She's not here. Her suffering is over now. You must accept her passing and go on with your life, as we all must." A tall and ruggedly handsome young man in his early twenties, Robert pulled his cloak a bit tighter as the wind picked up and the rain fell harder. The other mourners had walked away, leaving them isolated, piteous figures standing by the open grave. Two grimy laborers dressed in black waited under a nearby tree to fill the hole.

"If only I knew what happened."

"Mother, please, not here, not now. We'll find out, I promise." He knew the pledge was an empty one, but somehow he had to assuage her concerns, even if it meant lying.

Reluctantly, Vivian relented, and they slowly followed the others toward the waiting carriages and the house beyond.

*****

"He lived here for a long time before he died." Granger was concluding his genealogy lesson. Looking up from his daydreaming, he searched for Teresa. "Where are you?" Then, more loudly, "*Teresa!* Where are you hiding?"

"Here. I'm over here." Teresa stepped out from behind a cedar bush.

"Where were you? You wandered off."

"I just had the strangest experience."

"What are you talking about?"

Teresa thought for a moment. She wiped her forehead again and walked across a cracked sidewalk toward Granger. Trembling, she grabbed her right hand with her left and pulled both of them up against her body.

"I don't know. I've never felt anything like it. My...my fingers are tingling." Pointing feebly, she blurted out, "It was that grave over there, the one just sticking up above the ground." She reached out as she neared him, and, despite the heat, she pulled herself close. She felt breathless, and a pang of anxiety struck her chest.

"What's wrong, baby?" He could read the fear on her face.

"I can't...I don't know." She backed away and stared into Granger's eyes.

"What are you talking about?" asked Granger as he began walking in the direction Teresa had pointed.

"*No!* Don't go over there!" She was almost yelling, but he ignored her warning. "Is this it?" Granger looked down at the slab at his feet.

"Yes...yes."

After he read the inscription, he asked, "Okay, what happened?"

"I had some sort of vision, or maybe it was just a feeling. I can't say. But it sure was real."

"What kind of vision? What kind of feeling?"

"It was a scene, as if I were seeing what happened when she was buried. I know it sounds weird, but it was more than just a vision. I felt the sadness, the sorrow." Suddenly, she started to break down, the tears overflowing, pouring down her face.

"Stop. Don't say any more right now. Get hold of yourself. Let's get out of here. We can talk about it then."

Later, after Teresa had calmed down and they sat in a booth at a roadside café, Granger listened attentively as he swallowed an icy mouthful of tart lemonade.

"I...I don't really know what happened. Right after you started to talk about your great-grandfather, I saw that broken monument nearby. For some reason, it was intriguing to me, and I walked over to it. I read the inscription, and it reminded me of...well...of the baby and the accident. Our baby would've been her age now, you know." She squeezed her nose with a handful of tissue.

"Yes, I know." Granger diverted his eyes away from her. "Go on."

"Well, I could hardly read the inscription, so I ran my fingers over the letters to make it easier to make them out. That's when I saw this scene."

"You mean like a picture?"

"That's the weird part. It was as if I was watching a movie, but I...I felt the emotion too."

"I don't understand."

"Neither do I. I can't explain it." She dropped her head into her hand and closed her eyes.

"You have to try." There were only a few other people in the café and they seemed not to notice, but Granger stole a glance around their table to make sure. "Uh...keep your voice low."

Teresa ignored his warning. "I felt grief, overwhelming sadness, as if I were really *there*."

"Where is 'there'?"

"I don't know that either, but I think it was at the cemetery during the girl's funeral, like a hundred fifty years ago. The people were dressed in black. It was raining, and there were carriages nearby. There was an old lady wearing a bonnet. She was crying uncontrollably and looking at the grave. I got the impression she was the girl's mother. There was a young man with the old lady too, and he called her 'Mother'. He was trying to console her, but she wouldn't stop crying. That's what I saw." Teresa gulped down half her drink. "Now tell me how crazy I am."

"Crazy? No, you're not crazy." Teresa saw Granger wince and his eyes fill with compassion. "It was hot, and you were thinking about…about the accident. Maybe it was too much. I mean, the memories and all."

Teresa frowned and raised her voice. "No… *No*. It wasn't the heat." She saw a few heads turn to look at her, and she continued more softly. "I thought that too, at first. But, it was more than that. My fingers—the ones that touched the inscription—they tingled."

"Yeah. You told me. What do you mean they tingled?"

"They felt funny for a while, prickly all over, but now they're okay. And it was more than just a vision. I was part of it, like separated from here and now."

"Okay, okay, you had some sort of, well, 'experience'." Granger took a deep breath and squirmed. "Where do we go from here?"

"You're asking me?"

"Well, *you* had the vision. Do you want to just ignore it? We don't have to go back there…ever, if you don't want to. We can go home and pretend it never happened."

"But there's something else."

"There's more?"

She nodded. "There's a mystery—something about the girl's death that wasn't right. I don't know how she died, but it wasn't natural."

"You mean she was killed…murdered?"

"Maybe. I can't say, but it was part of the feeling I got."

Teresa saw both doubt and fear in Granger's eyes. She understood clearly the utter implausibility of her story, but at the same time she knew he would support her despite his misgivings.

Chapter Two

Jack McAlester sat glumly at his desk high in the Transamerica Tower and stared at the parting fog across the bay. The late morning sun was finally burning through the thick dampness that hugged the jagged coastline. In the distance he could see the terra cotta spires of the Golden Gate Bridge, and he could barely discern the Marin hills beyond.

"Jack, Linda's holding for you." Carol, his executive assistant for the past several years, jolted him out of his thoughts.

"Oh, okay. I'll get it," he replied as he turned away from the window and picked up the phone.

"Jack, I just wanted to tell you that I'll be out of pocket this evening: another one of those endless committee meetings. So, you'll have to fend for yourself tonight." Linda sounded breathless, as she always did.

"Oh. Well, I have a lot of work here anyway. Is Juanita lined up to stay with the kids?"

"Yes. Don't worry about them. And you can stay at work as long as you need to. Uh...another thing. The decorator was here this morning early and left some drawings of the remodel we talked about last week. If you get home before I do, I'd like for you to look them over. I'll leave 'em in the master. I told him we'd get back to him by Thursday."

"Thursday? That doesn't give us much time."

"I don't think it'll take long to discuss. He has wonderful ideas, and I just love them."

"Well, we need to look at more than just this one project. We need to consider everything we want to do to the house. I don't want to be remodeling everything twice. You know, this whole situation requires some coordination."

Linda protested, "Coordination? What do you mean? We talked about it."

"Now hold everything. Yes, we talked about it, but for only ten minutes. This thing needs a lot more than ten minutes' worth of discussion, especially at the prices *he's* charging."

"Jack, don't be difficult. I don't understand why you've been so hard to deal with lately."

"Listen. I'm not the one being difficult. *You* are. You're the one who wants to spend everything we have on some useless, overpriced renovations. What I'm saying is we need to look at our whole financial situation before committing to such a costly project. We've been spending way too much money on *everything* lately."

"We'll talk about this later. I gotta go." The phone went dead.

Jack felt dead too. The view from his office was one of the most breathtaking one could ever imagine, but he hardly noticed anymore. For most of the morning he had been staring at a blank computer screen thinking about composing a letter of resignation. Having invested fifteen years of his life at Todd Engineering, he was loath to leave, but he felt he had no recourse. The sad truth was that he knew the situation was mostly his own fault. Once a first-rate engineer, he had lost focus and had become a victim of his own success.

He glanced at the framed document hanging on the wall across from him: Master of Science in Engineering, *summa cum laude*, Stanford University. Despite geographic proximity, it had been a long way from the tile-roofed campus to the paneled office with the view of the scenic northern California seascape. He recalled his marriage to Linda ten years ago and the history since then. Within four years after they were married, they had produced the requisite son and daughter, and Linda had become well known in local society. Five years after that, Jack was promoted to Executive Vice President, the coveted office of the second in command. The promotions had been well earned. He had devoted himself to the company, frequently burning midnight oil to make sure his presentations were the most impressive. In every sense he went the extra mile and in every way he was rewarded. Yes, it had been difficult traversing the beautiful coastal hills between Palo Alto and San Francisco, but everyone both within and outside the company recognized that he was the heir-apparent who would one day occupy that even bigger office on the

next floor. The view from there was even better and so were the perks and the money.
Of late, however, the strain was beginning to show. His personal problems had led to sloppiness in the execution of his job, and several contracts under his supervision had been mishandled or lost entirely. Not only was his marriage in jeopardy, so also was his standing at Todd. In fact, his life was falling apart, and he was getting desperate.
Then, there was the letter. Jack really had no idea who sent it. He had almost thrown the thing away unopened because it seemed so out of place, so different. Unlike the other sleek, neatly printed pieces of mail, this envelope was tea-colored brown with frayed edges. The illegible original address had been crossed out and the office address was written in a much different script, as if the letter had been forwarded. He recalled the exchange with Carol when it appeared on his desk.

******

"Do you know anything about this letter?" Jack called to Carol in the next room.
"I can't keep up with *everything* around here. What're you talking about?"
"This envelope...it looks old. No return on it. And I can't read what's on the stamp or the postmark. It's addressed to San Francisco, but I can't figure out anything else. How did it end up here?" He examined it closely. "Must be a mistake."
Carol stuck her head in the door. "Let me see." Jack handed the unopened piece to her. "Maybe it's booby-trapped with some sort of explosive device. You think we should call the police or building security?" She fingered the paper and held it up to the light.
"Hmm. No. Give it to me." Too busy to worry about it at the time, he put it in the top drawer of his desk and soon forgot it.

******

Carol dropped another stack of mail onto his desk.
"Anything interesting?" asked Jack as he turned his attention from the blank computer screen.

A PEACE IN TIME

"Look at the top one," she said.

"Oh, another one of those strange envelopes." Jack rubbed his hand through his wavy black hair and stretched his six foot five frame against the back of his leather desk chair. He suddenly remembered the other letter and retrieved it from his desk drawer. "You know, these envelopes look the same, like they were mailed from the same place at the same time. I think we should open them. What do you think?"

"You *know* what I think. You've got my curiosity going," said Carol. She sat across from him as he gently slit open the edge of the first envelope. He pulled out a single piece of old paper that was almost as dingy as the envelope itself.

"Let's see here." Jack read it aloud.

> The time is right. Don't delay.
> Sarah B.

"Who's Sarah B.?" Carol wrinkled her forehead and squinted her eyes.

"I don't have any idea. Never heard the name." Jack stared absently across the room toward the wide window and the view across the bay as he scanned his memory.

"Open the other envelope," Carol said eagerly.

> Why have you not come? I am waiting.
> Sarah B.

"I don't get it." Carol frowned again. "These notes are really strange. Are you *sure* you've never heard of Sarah B.? I mean with you and Linda..."

Jack winced. "What do you know about Linda and me?"

"Oh, nothing." Despite her protestations, Jack knew busybody Carol was aware of his marital problems. "Just thought you might know who's sending these things. You know, office gossip and all."

"No. I'm telling you I don't know any Sarah B." He walked over to the window holding the last note. Even though he was sure he didn't know such a person, the name was somehow familiar, but he would never admit it to Carol. She would leap on such a confession.

Jack had forgotten about the resignation. The letters clearly intrigued him. "Carol, let me know if any more of these mysterious messages show up. If there *is* a next one, I want to open it right away."

******

Granger looked wistfully at the softly rolling East Texas hills that sprawled ahead of the car. "Beautiful, aren't they."
"What? What's beautiful?" responded Teresa. From her vantage point next to him in the front seat she could see he had that far-away look on his face again.
"The hills, the trees," Granger said as he shook his head slowly and smiled.
"You aren't thinking about when you were a kid again, are you?"
"So what's wrong with that?" Granger snipped.
"Nothing, I guess. But it's like you're in a trance when you get this way, and then you're depressed afterwards. You've been doing this sort of thing the whole twenty years we've been married."
"I just miss living around here sometimes. See that old barn over there?" He pointed toward a dilapidated structure with a tin roof. "That's one of old man Sheldon's barns. Used to have some horses in there. Seems like just yesterday."
"Umm."
"I walked along that blacktop over there almost every day. Boy, that stuff was hot during the summer. I had to be careful when I was barefooted."
"Yeah, yeah. You've told me that story before—several times."
"Well, it's a story that bears repeating." Granger looked at Teresa. He knew he was no longer that freckle-faced kid who drank cold sodas during the day and chased fireflies at night. Both time and Teresa had changed him, mostly for the better. Still, he couldn't quite let go.
"That's debatable," she countered. "You're treating everything around here just like your parents' house."
"What do you mean?" Granger bristled.
"You just won't let go. You should've sold that house years ago, but you haven't. You keep holding onto the past."
Granger started to bark back at her, but he reconsidered. "Well, this isn't the time or the place to discuss *that* subject again."
Teresa shook her head and turned away from him.

A PEACE IN TIME

After a moment of silence, Granger reached over and touched her left hand. "So, how are you feeling now? About this vision thing, I mean."

Her heart softened. "Oh, okay I guess. Just silly."

"Silly? Why?"

"You know...the fuss I made at the café. Maybe my so-called vision was just a bad mouthful of that pizza I ate last night."

"Why are you beginning to have second thoughts? The pizza theory is just as weird as the vision itself." Oops.

"*Weird?*"

"No, no. Not at all." He quickly fumbled for the right words to say. "I just think that, since the vision was so real to you, you shouldn't ignore it. That would be foolish."

Teresa thought for a moment. "Yeah. That's what I already said." Then, after a moment, "Do you have any idea how to look into it?"

Granger stroked his forehead and ran his hand down his face. "Well, we could see if there's some record of the dead girl in the county archives or maybe the report of her death in a newspaper...if there *was* any kind of newspaper around here a hundred fifty years ago. Oh, and we can try to find cemetery records."

"Okay. How do we go about getting information like that?"

"We should probably check the county courthouse first or maybe the county historical museum. I don't know exactly. It'll be a 'Sherlock Holmes experience'." Granger smiled at her, but secretly he knew how futile the effort would probably be. Though it was extremely unlikely that any records had survived, just making the effort might help to allay Teresa's anxiety.

******

The domed, sandstone-colored museum in the center of town had been the county courthouse for many years from the middle of the nineteenth century until well into the twentieth. The weathered statue of a Confederate soldier stood guard at the main entrance, his stiff hands clutching a bayoneted rifle, his cold eyes still defiantly searching for Yankee invaders. Several tiers of stone steps climbed to the hulking oak doors at the entrance, and, beyond, a large foyer led into a display area and a small office. Granger and Teresa knocked timidly on the office door.

From behind them, a soft wavering voice called out, "Can I help you?"

"Oh!" Teresa jumped. She smiled at the old man shuffling toward them and looked at him eye to eye. "I didn't know you were there."

"Sorry," he said as he adjusted his glasses.

"Uh, yes, I hope you can help us," said Granger. He looked down at the scrawny figure walking up to him.

"My name's Lawson...Ben Lawson." As he showed off a toothy grin, his dentures clicked. "Don't get many people 'round here these days, 'specially folks like you."

"Uh, my name's Granger Walker, and this is my wife Teresa. What do you mean 'like us'?" Granger frowned at him as he shook the shriveled hand he was offered.

"Mostly just get noisy school kids on field trips. You know." He chuckled, pulled out a wrinkled white handkerchief and wiped his nose.

"Oh. Yes, I suppose."

"Well, how can I help you?" He stuffed the handkerchief back into his pants pocket and smiled at Teresa.

"We're looking for some old death or cemetery records," said Granger.

"Old? How old? We don't have much back afore about 1900."

"Well, we need information from the mid-1800's."

He scratched his stubbly face. "Boy, that's way back. I don't know." Turning slowly and tottering through the display area, he waved his arm and ordered, "Come with me. We'll take a look."

Granger and Teresa dutifully followed him past cases full of discarded memories and unorganized heaps of dusty artifacts. Plows sat in one corner area, rifles in another. A pile of old porcelain dolls, their clothes in tatters, slumped nearby. Odd paintings and prints, framed newspaper articles and apothecary bottles lined the floor along another wall. The air was infused with a musty smell that triggered Teresa's recollection of the library in her grandparents' old house. After navigating around a large black carriage and down several small steps, they entered a room full of aging wooden file cabinets and shelving units.

"Here we are. The oldest stuff is in this room."

"Thank you, sir." Granger smiled. "Where would Balfour Cemetery records be?"

"Don't rightly know. Probably back in the corner over there." He stretched a shaking index finger in front of his bony face as he grinned back at Granger and winked at Teresa. "Just let me know when you finish."

Teresa turned to Granger after he had disappeared around the corner. "Boy, I don't know if this was such a good idea."

"Why?"

"Just seems creepy...that old man, this place." Then, disgustedly, "Why, he even *winked* at me."

Granger chuckled. "He's just old, not dead. What do you expect?" Then, more seriously, "As far as our being here, it's your vision, not mine."

"Thanks." Teresa gritted her teeth and turned away. She pulled out a couple of file drawers. "Well, let's get started. You take the first set of files, and I'll take the second. Okay?"

Time passed quickly as they rummaged through the old folders. A treasure-trove, the information was all from the early twentieth and late nineteenth century, and Granger couldn't help being fascinated by it all.

However, after an hour of searching, Granger was tiring of the exercise. Suddenly, he exclaimed, "Ah!"

"Did you find something?"

"Yeah. Here's someone with your maiden name."

Teresa dropped the papers she was holding. "Really? Feldkamp? There aren't many Feldkamps around. Let me see."

Thumbing through the file as quickly as she could, her eyes suddenly widened. Then she blinked deliberately several times as she ran her index finger along one of the fading lines on the paper. "Hey, this guy's name was Cecil Feldkamp. He was married to a woman named Martha, and he died in 1889. They had three children. Hmm...that's funny." She curled her bottom lip into her mouth and bit down gently. "I wonder. My dad's name was Cecil."

"You think you're related to the guy in the file?"

"Maybe. But, if I am, it'd be news to me."

"I thought all your relatives were originally from Arizona."

"Well, yes. My mother's relatives are, but about my dad's I don't know for sure. I seem to recall that some may have come from Texas, but it was never clear. And I certainly never remember anyone saying they were from around here." Teresa slumped back in her chair and felt another surge of empathy for Sarah. "Granger, do you think there might really be a connection between that girl buried out there in the cemetery and me?"

Granger arched his eyebrows and feigned a British accent. "I don't know, my dear. But, whatever is going on, it must be a deep, dark secret."

For the first time in a long while, a smile crept across Teresa's lips.

Chapter Three

"Quickly, Mother, quickly. The rain is coming down harder. You'll be drenched." Helped and hurried by her solicitous son, Vivian struggled into the waiting carriage. The light rain had turned into a steady downpour, some of which was starting to freeze. The breeze picked up as well, causing the smaller pines to bend. Her tears mixed with the rain on her cheeks and fell onto her black dress. Robert fought the umbrella, which was now of no practical use in the stiffening wind.

"To the house. Hurry!"

The driver snapped the whip and the horse lurched forward. Robert was almost thrown into the mud just as he was placing his foot onto the carriage step.

"Steady," the driver murmured while he pulled gently back on the reins.

Unconsoled, Vivian buried her head in Robert's shoulder.

"Mother, you must get hold of yourself. Think of appearances."

"But, why ... who? She was only a child."

"I don't know, but I'll do everything I can to bring the guilty to justice. Eventually, the monster will be found out."

"I think it was that gambler. I just know it."

"Someday, Mother, the truth will come out, no matter who it was."

The somber procession of carriages moved slowly toward the house beneath trees bowed as if in prayer.

******

Tears suddenly began to flow down Teresa's cheeks, and she wiped them off with her fist. "What's wrong?" Granger put his hand on her shoulder.

"It was a gambler." Teresa was almost sobbing. She pressed the ball of her right hand into each of her eyes and turned toward Granger. "She said it was a gambler...a gambler."

"What are you talking about? Why are you crying? Are you okay?"

"I don't know. I just had the feeling again. I was there again."

"There? You mean like at the cemetery?"

"Yes."

"Baby, you're scaring me. Are you sure?"

"I'm sure. It was the mother again. She said she thought it was the gambler who hurt her daughter."

"Who's the gambler?"

"She didn't say, but I think it's someone here, someone whose name is in these files. Why else would this have happened?" Teresa started to calm down, but she was still shaking. "That's really weird. It's like a dream, only I'm awake."

Granger shook his head. "Well, I think we should give this up. It's obviously too much for you, and I can't handle these visions of yours."

She grabbed his forearm. "No, no. Sarah, the young girl buried there, is still not at peace, and I can give her that peace. It's what I *have* to do." She paused, then continued, "You're much more analytical than I am, dear. So, I know it doesn't make any sense to you. It doesn't to me either. But you have to understand that I'm compelled to try to solve this...this mystery. " In some unfathomable way, she felt a connection between Sarah and the child who had been lost so many years ago. She couldn't help her own flesh and blood now, but maybe she could do something for this long-forgotten girl with whom she felt a strange but warm kinship.

Granger's lips became thin and tense, as they always did when he was about to disagree with her. Then, suddenly, his face relaxed, and he relented, "Okay, we'll go on, but it's against my better judgment. So what do we do now, in light of this most recent revelation?" Teresa felt relief, but she knew she needed Granger's support, and she had to make sure she did nothing that would risk losing it.

"I don't know exactly, but I'm certain of one thing," she said. "This Feldcamp guy we found in the records is somehow involved."

Time passed quickly as they gleaned every scrap of data about Cecil Feldkamp. Luckily, they were able to find records of deeds, bills of sale for land, even a reference to a brother named Lance.

The sun was dropping below the crest of Tucker Hill as they drove back through the brilliantly green countryside. Soon, the stars were twinkling overhead. Granger opened the moon roof and breathed in the warm, humid air filled with the faint scent of honeysuckle and freshly mowed grass. A smile grew across his face.

"Man, this brings back memories. I think you've stirred up the ages, dear, and it's spilling over onto me. You know, a long time ago, we used to catch fireflies...we called them lightning bugs...in a jar. We'd hang several jars from tree limbs and pretend they were lanterns. Then, when we were finished playing, we'd let them go. Sometimes we did that every night for a week, and I often wondered whether we caught the same ones over and over again. What do you think the chances of that are?"

Teresa wrinkled her forehead. "What a queer question. I don't know. Why would you think of that? It's so...uh...inconsequential."

"That's the point," said Granger. A lot of things are inconsequential, but we wonder about them anyway. Isn't this 'quest' of yours just like the fireflies: inconsequential? Isn't it just a fabrication that you should ignore? I don't think your visions are any more important than the nostalgia I have for my childhood. Nevertheless, they're important to *you*."

Teresa drew her arm away. "No. It's real. I can't ignore it." She dropped her head and thought for a moment. Then she said tearfully, "I thought you were with me on this."

"That's just the point, honey. I *am* with you, and you're in the here and now. You're not some 'channel' from the past to the present. You're my wife, and you live in the *twenty-first* century, not in the nineteenth. I know I need to let go of a lot of things that happened to me out there in that countryside years ago, too. I haven't been totally successful in doing that yet, but I'm working on it. So, are you *sure* you don't need to let this mystery thing go too? Is it all that important?"

"Yes, dear, I'm sure. Now, let's go back out to the cemetery and see if we can find the graves of any of the people we found out about in the files."

A PEACE IN TIME

In truth, the searing logic of Granger's words was crystal clear to Teresa, but she couldn't bring herself to admit it. Her head was telling her he was right, that she should abandon this obviously errant search. The visions should indeed be inconsequential, but her heart was screaming for satisfaction. She felt inexorably tied to this long-ago event, and she knew that the bond could be broken only by a final resolution of the mystery.

******

"No, no." Vivian groaned in her sleep. "Sarah...Sarah, where are you? I can't see you anymore."

"Miss Vivian. Ma'm. Wake up. You dreamin'." A house servant gently shook the tossing figure in the four-poster bed. "Wake up."

Vivian writhed under the soft white sheets and tossed her head right and left. The servant grabbed her hands and pressed them down onto the pillow. "You dreamin', ma'm."

Suddenly Vivian's eyes sprang open, and she stopped mid-groan. Breathing heavily, she shook her head and blinked deliberately. "Oh, oh, Carrie, I...I'm sorry. I didn't mean to cause a ruckus." Gradually she began to calm down and Carrie released her grip. "Give me my kerchief, Carrie. I need to sit up a minute and catch my wind."

Carrie opened a drawer in the small mahogany table near the bed where the lighted candle flickered. Fishing out a lace handkerchief, she turned and smiled at the wan figure in the bed.

Once the belle of every party from Shreveport to Natchez and on to New Orleans, Vivian had in her early years visited the plantations of relatives all along the Mississippi and up the Red during the summer and had spent winters at her father's home near Jefferson. When in New Orleans, she practiced her French in the shops of only the best milliners and dressmakers. But those days were long past now, and sometimes she could hardly remember them. Vivian had all the right bloodlines, and she had married well. During a ten-year period, she gave birth six times, but only two, Robert and Sarah, had survived infancy. The mistress of the house, she ruled with a firm but gentle hand. The slaves and house servants loved her, particularly at Christmas, when she was especially generous to them. After her husband died in a riding accident, she shouldered well the full responsibility of running the plantation.

Since Sarah's death, however, her mood had changed dramatically. She angered easily, and no one could quite satisfy her needs, much less her wants. What was once quite good enough now had to be perfect, errors that at one time had engendered only a gentle reprimand resulted in expulsion from the house, and she was beginning to enforce corporal punishment for repeated offenses. Her personality had changed. She now harbored a deep-seated, inner anger. Her handling of the business of the plantation had suffered as well. The family fortune, once ample, was now shrinking. Her life, once blessed and tranquil and magical, lay dead with Sarah in the grave.

Vivian blew her nose and placed the handkerchief under her pillow.

"You all right, ma'm?"

"Yes...yes, I'm all right. Go back to bed, Carrie. Don't mind me. I was just having a nightmare. Leave the candle on the table there and go back to bed."

Carrie smiled and silently closed the bedroom door behind her. Vivian lay staring at the orange flame. In the dim flickering light broad shadows of the furniture danced along the walls. Sarah had danced too, but, like the movement of the shadows, she was now just an illusion, her life force existing only in Vivian's memory. The bedroom down the hall had been Sarah's. Now locked, its door was the portal through which Sarah had passed so many times. She had struggled to push open the heavy piece of carved oak when she was small and had bolted through it when she was older. Her laughter was the glow of a thousand candles, illuminating the darkness in the hearts of everyone who knew her. Vivian couldn't help picturing her in the blue satin dress, her favorite, the one she was wearing that terrible night. A tear traced the crease in Vivian's cheek and dropped silently onto the crisp white sheet. Wretchedly, she began to sob.

Chapter Four

The plane carrying Jack southeastward floated softly far above the Llano Estacado, the treeless high plains of West Texas. An endless patchwork of irrigated cotton fields and expansive cattle ranches sprawled below him like some borderless quilt. Jack could barely make out the web of highways that ran between the small towns and the grid of lease roads that marked the massive oil fields.

As Jack stared at the canvas below him, he wondered why he was making this trip. The cryptic notes from "Sarah B." haunted his dreams at night and his thoughts during the day despite his efforts to ignore them. Three more had arrived over the past few days, the last one directing him to an obscure small town in East Texas.

Come to me. The road is long to Texas, but I am still here in Balfour.
Please...I await.
Sarah B.

He had agonized over whether to act on the instructions. Paying so much attention to the mysterious messages was not at all like him, the practical number-crunching engineer. In truth, however, the trip was a convenient escape. For a few days he wouldn't have to contend with his problems at the office and at home. He recalled the strained discussion he had had with Linda just before he left.

******

"I'll be gone on a business trip for the next few days."
"Oh? Where are you going this time?"
"Houston."

"Houston? I don't recall that you've ever been there before."

"No, I haven't. In fact, I've never been to Texas at all. It'll be a trip of discovery."

"Hmm...well, what am I supposed to do about the tickets we have for the symphony tomorrow night?"

Jack bristled. "Somehow, I think you'll find someone to go with. My being gone shouldn't present a problem."

"You're right. It probably won't."

"And it never has."

******

North of Houston's serpentine ribbons of concrete, the highway wound its way over gently rolling hills and through thick forests broken by wide fields and small farms. Jack had never thought that any part of Texas would be so lush. His concept of the state was that of the Old West, with cactus and dust and mammoth boulders used as cover by masked bandits. He could picture all the characters in a shoot-out, the bad guys exchanging gunshots with the posse of white-hatted deputies. It was a Saturday morning cowboy serial all over again: Hopalong Cassidy, Roy Rogers and Bob Steele. But *this* Texas was different, bucolic and verdant, with not a bandit in sight.

A few hours after leaving Houston, a green highway sign directed him toward a narrow but well-kept farm-to-market road that burrowed like a tunnel through clusters of towering pines. As he steered the car in the direction of Balfour, Jack recalled how difficult it was to hide the real reason for this trip from Carol.

******

"Carol, I need to meet with some people in Houston. Could you get me a flight reservation for tomorrow?"

"Sure. What about a return flight?"

"Uh...I don't know how long I'll be there, so leave the return open." He knew she would be skeptical because he never did anything without a fully developed flow chart, and that included trip planning.

"No date for a return? What's wrong with you?"

"Oh, this thing just came up, so I don't have all the details yet."

Carol raised her eyebrows and tilted her head in disbelief. "Okay, if you say so."

******

He really didn't know how long he would be gone. At least that much was true. Soon he was in Balfour, which consisted of a general store, a post office, a gas station and a few houses in desperate need of new paint.

"Can I help you?" drawled a fifty-something lady behind the counter in the ramshackle store. She smiled genuinely as she tossed back her graying hair.

"I hope so, but I'm not sure. I'm doing some genealogy work, looking for some ancestors who might have lived in the area. Who around here would be the best person to talk to about something like that?"

"You're in luck. That someone's me. I'm Joyce Winstead." She offered her right hand. "I've lived around here all my life, and my family's been here for over a hundred years. Who're you looking for?"

"My name is McAlester, Jack McAlester, and I'm looking for...."

"Never heard of any McAlesters, and you don't sound like you're from anywhere near here."

"I'm from San Francisco, and the ancestors I'm looking for might have a different last name. I don't really know what name I'm searching for, but I do know the last name that starts with the letter 'B'. All I know is there's a Sarah B."

Joyce stared blankly at a point across the room, as if she were looking at some yellowed, dusty list that had been filed away long ago. "B...hmm. Well, that'd fit several families—Brown, Blivens, Bonny, uh...Best, Bollinger, Boyington. And I may have missed a couple. Some of them still have people living here, some not. And Sarah...that's been a fairly common name over the years. When did this Sarah B. live around here?"

"Don't know that either, but I think it was years and years ago."

"Not much help." She shook her head. "You might want to take a walk through the cemetery. Maybe you'd find some names there that'd point you in the right direction." She was smiling again.

"Cemetery. Yeah, that's an idea. Where is it?"

"Just down the road." She pointed east as she walked toward the front door. "There's a sign about a mile that way, then two miles off to the right on a narrow blacktop. It's old. Probably the earliest grave is from the 1830's. If you find a name that tickles your fancy, it'd at least be a start."

The sky was growing dark with clouds and the wind swirled through the parking lot outside the cyclone fence that surrounded the cemetery as Jack walked toward the heavy gate at the entrance. He shook his head and thought about his predicament. Here he was, half a continent away from home, in some dusty corner of history, at a place he had never heard of, all based upon instructions contained in mysterious notes sent directly from the unknown. Surely he had better things to do with his time and much more important issues to address. What level of embarrassment would he suffer if all of this leaked out to his wife, to his co-workers and, perhaps most important of all, to company management? His career, what was left of it, would evaporate like a will-o'-the-wisp into the ethereal solitude of the East Texas piney woods. He could hear the talk now: "Jack's gone off the deep end. We wouldn't want someone like him even associated with Todd, much less in the top job." Yes, all of this would have to be kept secret. No one must find out.

******

Some distance away in another part of the cemetery, Granger and Teresa heard the gate open and saw the tall, well-dressed figure heading in their direction. Suddenly a lightening flash and a clap of thunder startled them. Just as quickly, huge raindrops started falling and the wind heaved.

"Let's get under something, quick," ordered Granger. He looked around and pointed. "This way."

Pulling Teresa along, he ran to one of the miniature Parthenons, and they cowered under the granite roof as the rain fell harder. At the other end of the cemetery, Jack sought shelter too. Seeing the same shelter, he ran quickly through the now torrential downpour and, dripping, huddled next to them.

While the heavy rain continued to fall and the thunder rumbled, Teresa looked at the stranger next to them. They didn't speak, but Jack smiled at her. Teresa thought how incredibly handsome this stranger was—tall like Granger, with an even stronger, more athletic profile. But there was something else that attracted her, and it wasn't his looks. She felt a strange rush of déjà vu, and she couldn't keep her eyes off him. Finally, after the rain subsided, Teresa offered a smile and blurted almost unconsciously, "Don't I know you?"

Granger's eyes widened as he turned to her. "You know this man?"

Almost monotonically, she replied, "In fact, somehow I think I do."

Granger squirmed and moved closer to her while extending his hand to Jack. "Uh, my name's Granger Walker, and this is my wife Teresa." Teresa's face was still blankly transfixed.

"I'm Jack McAlester. Guess we were lucky to find the same shelter. Quite a downpour." He pulled out a handkerchief to wipe the water dripping from his face.

"You're here looking for someone," said Teresa.

"Why, yes. How did you know?"

"And you've come a long way."

Jack shook his head. "Right again. I'm from San Francisco."

Granger stuttered, "Uh...maybe we...uh...need to get out of here and go somewhere we can talk."

Jack looked into Teresa's eyes but quickly turned away. "Yes, yes, I agree. A rational discussion—that's what we need."

Taking Teresa's cold, wet hand, Granger walked toward the gate. "Are you all right?" he asked after they closed the car doors.

"I'm okay." But she added, "I'm just a little woozy." She had no idea what had come over her. Jack was a masculine personification of temptation, and her attraction to him was immediate and overwhelming.

Taken aback by his wife's reaction to the stranger, Granger recoiled. "Yeah, well, I kind of feel the same way,"

******

At a café down the road, Granger and Teresa exchanged stories with Jack, and they concluded there could be a connection between Jack and the mystery.

"I'm stumped," said Jack as he sipped on a foamy glass of cold beer. "I know of nothing that would link this Sarah Bollinger to me or any ancestor of mine." He sat against the back of the booth and fingered his half-empty glass. "And this thing is getting *weirder* all the time. Was it just luck that we ran into one another today?"

"Maybe, maybe not," said Granger. "I've been really skeptical from the start, but I confess I can't explain away the coincidence."

"Of course, you must know I *am* relieved a bit," said Jack.

"How so?"

"At least I'm not alone. I mean, now I know I'm not having some kind of *solitary* Twilight Zone experience."

Feeling a bit more comfortable with the situation, Granger chuckled. "And even if you *are* crazy, you know there are at least a couple of other people who're just as bad off."

"I guess you could say that."

Teresa was unusually quiet.

"You okay, dear?" asked Granger.

"Okay? Yes, I think so." In truth, the world had turned upside down. Jack was still wet from the soaking rain, his shirt plastered to his skin. She traced his arms and chest with her eyes and looked up into his ruggedly tanned face lined with slight creases in all the right places. She examined his dark hair and brown eyes and the large hands that surrounded rather than just held the glass in front of him. Still struggling to squelch any obvious signs of her feelings, she wondered whether Jack felt the same.

"You don't look okay," replied Granger.

Teresa thought she saw a hint of suspicion on Granger's face, and she suddenly felt a surge of emotion. "Granger, I...I'm not sure I can handle this much longer." This time the emotion was fear, not of the visions, but of her own desires.

Obviously misinterpreting her comment, Granger replied, "I know, honey, but what's our alternative? Just walk away and pretend nothing has happened?"

Teresa composed herself. "You mean treat it like the lightning bugs?"

"Lightning bugs? What do you mean?" Jack was puzzled.

She just couldn't let Granger know what she was thinking about Jack. "It's an inside joke," said Teresa. "I'm ready to do almost anything. I know these people have been dead for a long time, but they're not really at rest. And, for some reason, I won't be able to rest either until we figure this thing out."

"Well," Jack suggested, "we can go talk to that lady at the store in Balfour. Maybe she can tell us something now that we have some names."

******

Joyce contorted her face as she thought. "Sarah Bollinger. Bollinger. That last name's very familiar, but this Sarah...that's way back. No more Bollingers around here anymore. The last one moved away maybe fifty years ago, when I was a little girl. Most of 'em moved to Mississippi, I think. The father's first name was Richard...or maybe Robert."

"Robert? That's one of the Feldkamp names we found at the library." Teresa was exultant.

"Don't get too excited. Robert's a pretty common name," said Jack.

Joyce's eyes lit up. "Feldcamp. Now, *there's* a name I know well."

"Really? What do you know about *them*?"

"Well, there were a lot of Feldcamps living around here at one time. They intermarried with the old settlers, but most of them left a long time ago too. Only one still around here now: old Jed Feldcamp. He lives in a trailer up near Pepper Creek Road."

"Where did the Feldcamps that moved away go?" Teresa was even more curious.

"Out west, I think. Some to California, some to Arizona."

"Arizona? That's where my mother's from. She met my dad there, but maybe his ancestors were from here. I think it may all be coming together."

"It's still circumstantial, but these pieces seem to fit," said Granger. "Maybe we need to go see Jed."

"Might be a good idea," said Joyce. "But be careful."

"Why?" asked Teresa.

"Well, he's kind of hard to deal with. You know, sort of a hermit."

"Great. We're going to try to get facts from a guy who doesn't want to talk to us." Jack shrugged and shook his head.

"We'll do whatever we have to. He may not be perfect, but he is a source. Maybe we'll catch him on one of his nice days." At least Granger was optimistic.

Chapter Five

Jed Feldcamp's dilapidated trailer sat next to a small stagnant pond that overflowed into Pepper Creek. Clay pots of various sizes containing withered plants sat sadly on the small concrete porch, and a solitary deck chair with a torn canvas seat slouched next to Jed's old rusting Impala.

"Mr. Feldcamp?" asked Teresa as she stared at the grizzled, sixtyish face through the screen door.

"Yeah. What d'ya want?" Jed was gruff and frowning, almost belligerent.

"I...uh...we'd like to talk to you about some of your ancestors. My name is Teresa Walker, but my maiden name was Feldcamp. This is my husband Granger and Mr. McAlester."

"So?"

"So...so, we'd like to ask you a few questions."

"I don't answer any questions these days. Don't have no use for people."

"Well, we don't want to disturb you, but we need your help to solve a mystery."

"Mystery? Must be *your* mystery. Sure to hell not mine. Now, get your damned ass off my property. I don't want to talk to anybody." He slammed the door shut.

Granger broke the silence as the trio stood staring at one another. "Guess I was wrong. It's not one of his nice days."

"I don't think he has any nice days," offered Jack.

During their drive back to Balfour, Teresa waxed optimistic. "You know, Joyce told us Jed used to be a pretty successful business man, but he kind of resigned from accepted society several years ago when he couldn't handle all the social changes going on in the world."

"Yeah, so?" asked Granger.

"Well," replied Teresa, "I'm not totally giving up on old Jed. We can probably reach him...eventually. And I have a feeling there's some information we can get from him. We just need some twist to our approach."

"What kind of twist?" asked Granger.

"Oh, I'm not sure, but no matter. It'll all come together eventually. You'll see. Remember, I'm the clairvoyant one."

Granger chuckled, and the laughter spilled over to Jack.

"Boy, it's been a long time since I've laughed like this," said Jack. He yawned. "You know, I just realized how tired I am, what with the drive from Houston and all. Why don't we call it a day? I have a hotel room reserved in Tyler."

Teresa reacted instantly. "You don't have to drive all that way, Jack. Why don't you stay with us at Granger's parents' old house? It's not much but it's only about ten miles down the road."

Granger interjected nervously, "Well, the place *is* pretty small, dear. Maybe Jack would be more comfortable at a hotel. We can arrange to meet him tomorrow."

"Don't be silly," said Teresa. Then, turning toward Jack, "You just *have* to stay with us. We could use the time to get to know you better. Maybe we can even come up with some more information that could help us with this crazy mystery."

Jack didn't hesitate. "Well, I confess I'm tired enough not to protest. Just show me where I can curl up for the night and I'll be out like a light."

Granger wasn't happy. He hardly spoke while they drove back to the cemetery to let Jack pick up his car. He couldn't help feeling that this whole thing would not end well. The immediate connection between Teresa and Jack was obvious, and Granger bristled silently. The sun was still just above the western horizon as they entered the driveway at the old Walker family home, a small white frame structure that had been built in the thirties.

"It's only got two bedrooms and two baths. I grew up here. I've been meaning to get rid of it since my parents died, but I confess I've had a hard time facing that prospect. You know how it is."

"Yeah," said Jack, though he really didn't quite understand.

Granger continued, "We live in Dallas, and we're here only once in a long while."

"Yes, and the place really needs some repair work," said Teresa.

"I'll turn the air conditioner up," said Granger as they entered through the back door. "You can put your things in the front bedroom. That used to be my room when I was a kid." He pointed Jack down a narrow wallpapered hallway.

"I'll see what I can scrape together for some sort of meal," offered Teresa.

Later, over a rather eclectic dinner, they got to know each other better.

"It's strange," said Jack. "I only met you both today, but, for some reason, it feels as if I've known you for a long time."

"I feel the same way," offered Teresa.

Granger interjected, "Well, sometimes people just seem to connect for no apparent reason. You know. Uh...you married, Jack?"

"Why, yes. Been married about ten years and have two kids. In fact, I have the obligatory picture here in my billfold."

"Nice looking kids, and your wife is beautiful. It must be wonderful living in San Francisco. What a gorgeous place. Of course, we've only been there a couple of times. Mostly I remember the fog."

"And I remember the shopping," Teresa said as she smiled and handed the pictures back to Jack.

"Yeah...well...San Francisco is certainly famous for its fog. It's great, but I dare say it's more attractive to visitors than to residents. Don't get me wrong. I like living there and all that, but it's expensive, and from where I live the commute is awful."

"I guess you've heard more jokes than you want to hear about the 'fruits and nuts' out there," said Granger.

"Oh yeah, and I suppose we have more than our fair share."

"And what do you do for a living?"

"I'm an engineer, a VP at Todd Engineering. We construct bridges and such. What do you do, Granger?"

"I'm a writer, mostly magazines. I'm pretty much retired now, though. I do some freelance work occasionally."

"Teresa, what about you?"

"Part time, substitute teaching."

"Tell me about your wife, Jack," said Granger.

"Well, she's really into volunteer work. She serves on several charity committees. You know...feed the hungry, clothe the naked. And, there are the kids. Lots to do." Jack fingered his glass nervously and took a bite out of a chocolate chip cookie.

Teresa looked down at her plate. "We always wanted to have a family. In fact, we *did* have one child, but she died when she was a baby, about eighteen years ago. We wanted more, but no luck, and my biological clock stopped ticking quite a few years ago." She stole a quick glance at Granger, but he seemed to be looking away from her.

"Well, ours weren't exactly planned," said Jack. The silence afterward was broken only by the soft hum of the window air conditioner. "Uh...I think I should probably call home and let Linda know where I am."

"Of course. In the meantime, Granger and I will clean up this mess."

******

"Hello."

"Oh, where are you? Haven't heard from you since you left, and you've had your cell turned off."

"Yes. Well, I've been busy. I'm in Houston. I have a meeting tomorrow, but it may run over another day or so."

"You don't know when you'll be back here?"

"No. Not yet. Uh...I'll call you."

"Well, just remember we have that reception on Sunday. You need to be back for that."

"Reception?"

"Yes. You don't remember? I told you about it several times, and I know it's on your calendar."

"Oh, yeah...the Berkeley reception."

"That's the one. It's at five."

"I'll try to make it."

"You better do more than just try. It's important."

"Uh...okay. Are the kids all right?"

"They're fine I guess."

"What do you mean 'I guess'?"

"Juanita's been with them all day. I just got back to the house and haven't seen them yet."

"Well, they're going to start thinking Juanita's their mother."

"Jack, don't be silly. I'm busy just like you. Everything here is okay. Where are you staying?"

"Oh, well...I'll be moving hotels, so just call my cell if you need to get hold of me."

"You have to have it on, you know."

"Yeah, yeah. Talk to you later."

"Bye."

Jack threw the cell phone down hard on the pillow and slammed his right fist into his left palm. He picked up his suitcase, dropped it onto the bed, and then stood for a moment shaking his head before unlocking the zipper to remove the clothes he would need for the night.

Teresa and Granger were both exhausted when they retired to the master bedroom, Granger's parents' room since he was a boy. Small family photos crowded the top of the long oak dresser, and other larger pictures covered one wall of the room. Teresa always felt weird when she and Granger made love because she could just imagine his parents doing the same thing. She remembered Granger telling her a story about the room being locked on several occasions when he was very young and, later, his speculating about what was going on behind that bolted door.

"Jack seems really nice," said Teresa as she slipped under the covers.

"Yes, he does *seem* nice."

"I think he's a little lonely."

"Lonely? How can you tell?"

"I don't know. Just the way he talks. He's not very open about his family life. Must be something going on there."

"You're either imagining things or you're being clairvoyant again."

"No. Just intuitive."

"Well, you better be more concerned about this mystery than about Jack's private life. We just met him, you know. He could be a complete phony."

Teresa answered almost without thinking. "Phony? No. No way. He's for real."

"Real? Well, so am I." Granger pulled Teresa toward him and gave her a long kiss. "Baby, I know Jack's a handsome guy, and he's got a great personality. Just remember: you belong to me."

Teresa smiled. "Good night, dear."

"Night."

******

Jack squinted at the crimson numbers on the digital clock beside his head. It was two thirty. Although he had fallen asleep quickly, he awoke soon afterwards. Thoughts raced through his mind: Linda, the kids, his career, the letters, the cemetery, Teresa and Granger. Too many things were going on for even his well-evolved brain to process. Though the white noise of the air conditioner was louder than most of the other night sounds, he could occasionally hear the lilting call of a bird, sometimes quite close to the house, sometimes far away. After listening for a while, he put on his robe and tiptoed outside to the front porch.

The darkness was alive with activity. Crickets, cicadas, owls, frogs and that solitary bird filled the warm, heavy air with sound. The sky was a starscape, the Milky Way a transparent fog arching overhead. Because he lived near the city, Jack had hardly ever seen such a display of heavenly splendor. The scent of sweet honeysuckle and of pungent pine, both unfamiliar aromas, infused his senses. This was a completely new experience, and it was strangely refreshing, as if he were on a different planet, light years away from the earth with which he was accustomed. He leaned up against a porch post and drank it all in.

"Can't sleep?" asked a soft voice.

He jumped reflexively. "Teresa. What are you doing up? You scared me."

She adjusted the belt of her short robe that only slightly covered a thin nightgown.

"I couldn't sleep either. Sometimes I come out here during the night to get rid of the cobwebs."

"That's what I needed to do too."

She could see small droplets of sweat forming across Jack's forehead. "What's the matter? I detected something when we were talking at dinner."

"Nothing...nothing. Just a lot of things are going on. You know...the mystery and all." He ran his hand across his brow.

"I think it's something more than that," said Teresa.

"Uh...no...no." He turned away from her and stared out into the darkness.

She stepped toward him and gently touched his right arm. "Jack, somehow I think there's a bond...there's some tie between us." She was totally out of her element. How could she feel such a connection with this man she had just met? How could she be so unfaithful to Granger? She felt a sudden kinship with all those errant lovers in fiction who, inexplicably, fall for each other at first sight. She had always thought those characters were just that—fiction. She had never considered that she could become one of *them*.

Turning toward her again, he replied, "I feel it too, but it isn't rational. I mean, we don't really know each other."

"You're right. But, sometimes things just aren't rational. On occasion, things happen, like these visions of mine. They aren't rational either, but they *are* real." She couldn't believe what she was saying.

"Maybe. But I'm too much of an engineer to be convinced of that just yet."

"Don't you know there are some things you just can't prove, but nevertheless they're real? What about love, for instance. You can't prove it, but it's a fact. People love each other. Right?"

"Right."

"You love your wife. Right?"

"Uh...yes."

Teresa raised her eyebrows and continued, "So you must be able to accept some sort of connection between us."

"Well, when you put it that way...."

Jack took her hand and squeezed the fingers gently, looked into her eyes and drew her toward him. "Teresa, I...."

Just at that moment a cluster of fireflies appeared buzzing around the porch. Teresa blinked and stared at them for an instant. "Jack, we shouldn't. We...."

"Right. Right." He released her and leaned back up against the post as that same solitary bird called out from a nearby pine tree. "Uh, what do you call that bird?" he asked.

"A whippoorwill. It's a whippoorwill."

Chapter Six

The aroma of steaming coffee wafted like the sound of a charmer's flute from the kitchen to Jack's bedroom. He was awake again, but this time he felt rested. Most of the babble in his head during the night was now replaced by thoughts of eggs, bacon, toast and that wonderful, beckoning coffee.

"Good morning. Did you sleep okay?" Granger was attending to an egg on the griddle as Jack walked into the kitchen.

"Pretty good. I guess the time difference got to me a little, but I feel rested now."

"Great. Well, first things first: You want eggs and bacon?"

"That'd be great. And some coffee."

"Right over there." Granger pointed toward a steaming carafe on the counter.

"Where's Teresa?"

"Still asleep. I guess she was more exhausted than I was."

Jack was eager to pursue the mystery. "Well, today we could try to talk to old hermit Jed again, perish the thought. *Or* we could go see that lady at the store, or even just go back to the cemetery and wait for another one of Teresa's visions."

Granger grimaced at the thought of yet another vision. "Yeah. But I have an alternative plan. We could just stay here in the AC and watch baseball on TV. I think the Giants might be playing today."

Jack smiled back as he poured the hot, dark liquid into a mug. "As attractive as that sounds, it wouldn't help us solve the mystery. I can't stay here very long, you know." He hesitated a moment, and then continued, "In fact, my wife doesn't even know where I am."

"Where does she think you are?"

"In Houston at a business meeting."

"If I might ask, why wouldn't you tell her?"

"Well, it's hard to explain. Let's just say that she wouldn't understand. She doesn't know anything about the letters either."

Granger frowned. "Hmm."

"Well, there's more to it than that," Jack quickly added.

"You guys already up?" Teresa, dressed for the day, was trying to stifle a yawn as she walked into the room.

"What do you mean *already*? It's getting late," objected Granger.

"Ugh. I need coffee," she said.

"We all do," responded Jack. He glanced up at Teresa from where he was sitting, and she smiled.

Suddenly, there was a knock at the front door. "Now who could that be at seven thirty in the morning?" asked Teresa.

An attractive late middle-aged woman stood on the porch. As she opened the door, Teresa's first thought was that the well-dressed redhead with perfect hair and makeup in front of her must have been an actress or model at one time.

"Are you Mrs. Walker, Mrs. Teresa Walker?"

"Why, yes."

"My name is Henrietta Caldwell. I live a few miles down the road. I apologize for coming by so early, but I have some information that I think you might be interested in having right away. I'm driving to Dallas today, and I'll be out of town for about a week. I just didn't think it would wait 'til I get back."

"Why don't you come in, Mrs., or Ms...."

"It's *Mrs.* Caldwell."

"Pardon me a minute. I'll be right back." Teresa retrieved Granger and Jack from the kitchen and introduced them to the visitor.

"I knew you when you were a boy, but you may not remember me. I was a few years ahead of you in school," said Henrietta to Granger.

"Why, yes, I remember you. Good to see you again. It's been a very long time." Granger was quickly sifting through dusty memories, but he couldn't quite recall her.

"Would you like some coffee, Mrs. Caldwell?" asked Teresa.

"Oh, no thanks. I have a long drive ahead of me, and I've had enough already. And please call me Henrietta." She paused for a moment. "Again, let me apologize for coming unannounced. You don't have a phone here and I didn't know your cell number, so I had to drop by in person. Anyway, I understand from Joyce Winstead down at the store that you're looking for information about the Bollinger and Feldcamp families."

"Why, yes. I guess word does get around," said Teresa. "You know Balfour's a small town. News travels fast."

"What kind of information do you have, uh...Henrietta?"

"Well, my mother passed away several years ago, but she knew some of the Bollingers before they moved and she knew Jed Feldcamp when he was young. In fact, she used to baby-sit him. Well, I just happened to remember something my mother told me about Jed and the Feldcamps."

"Oh, what's that?"

"I know this is a minor thing, but I thought, well...if you're looking for any information at all.... Jed...he has a birthmark."

"Birthmark? What do you mean?"

"It's a really distinctive discoloration on the skin. It wouldn't be that important, but my mother said most all the Feldcamps have it. Jed sure does. My mother saw it every time she changed his diaper. Silly how you remember things, isn't it?"

Granger and Teresa looked at each other.

"What does the birthmark look like?" asked Teresa.

"Well, I know this sounds strange, but it's sort of like a target...you know, several circles with the same center, and about an inch across." Henrietta hesitated. "I was reluctant to come by to tell you about it. Seems so...unimportant. But, for some reason, I felt compelled. Can't explain it."

Teresa was wide-eyed and speechless. "Uh..."

Granger quickly interjected, "We really appreciate your coming by to tell us. It could be significant. Any clue we can find, you know."

"Oh, yes...and the Bollingers. There's something about them too. Well, they're one of the really old families. The old Bollinger home place is up the road about five miles. They lived around here for way over a hundred years before the last Bollinger moved away, and there are lots of Bollingers buried out in the old cemetery."

"Yes, we know."

"Well, seems there was some sort of vendetta between the Bollingers and the Feldcamps."

"Vendetta?"

"You know...a feud, like the Hatfields and McCoys. It'd been going on for generations."

"What was the basis of the vendetta?" Granger felt his heart start pumping faster.

"That part was never really clear, at least not to my mother. Rumor was that it had to do with some murder, or some suspicion of a murder, of a Bollinger by a Feldcamp. If it really did happen, it was never resolved."

"Do you know any particular names of those who were involved?"

"No, but it must've been a very long time ago, way before anybody my mother knew was born. Lots of the details were lost over the years, but I remember my mother said it was particularly gruesome. The Bollingers around in my mother's time might never have known the details themselves."

Teresa sat back on the couch and tried to drink it all in. "What else?"

"Oh, that's all. It's not much. And, like I said, I didn't know whether I should come by at all."

"You've given us a lot to think about, Henrietta," said Teresa. "A lot."

"Well, I must be going. Like I said, I have an appointment at noon in Dallas."

"Uh...thanks again for coming by," said Granger. "You don't know how helpful this is."

After Henrietta left, they all retreated back into the kitchen to consider the bombshell that had just been dropped on them. Both Granger and Teresa were shaken.

"The vendetta stuff was interesting, but I had to keep from laughing about the birthmark," said Jack.

"Don't laugh, Jack. I have a birthmark like that," said Teresa as she rolled up her right sleeve to reveal the discoloration at the top of her arm.

"What?" Jack's eyes widened as he started to feel the gravity of the information that they had just been given.

"More evidence that I'm related to the Feldcamps from around here."

"Pretty strong evidence, I'd say," said Granger. "What's the chance that Teresa would have a similar birthmark without being related?"

"Almost zilch. I'd say this nails it." The analytical part of Jack's brain was trying to grasp the mathematics of it all.

"What about this murder...and the vendetta?" Teresa felt her hands go cold. "Granger, I'm really scared now. I think this whole thing is for real. I think Sarah Bollinger was murdered by a Feldcamp who was one of my ancestors."

Granger cautioned, "Let's not get carried away, dear. While I agree it all seems to fit, we still have only sketchy evidence. Do you *really* think we're dealing with a murder that was perpetrated a hundred and fifty years ago?"

"Yes. Maybe. Isn't that what all of this is pointing to?"

"Well, yeah. But...."

"If I can get a word in," said Jack, "I tend to agree with Teresa, but I still don't know why I might be involved. I got these notes, but we don't have any information linking me to Sarah Bollinger *or* the Feldcamps."

"Obviously we don't have all the answers yet," said Granger. "All we have are some clues."

"Clues and a lot of fear," added Teresa. "So, where do we go from here?"

Teresa's eyes lit up. "Why don't we check out the old Bollinger mansion? Henrietta said it's nearby."

"Yeah, but how would we get in and what would we be looking for? We don't even know who lives there now," said Granger.

"Well, maybe Joyce could help us out with that," said Jack. "She knows everybody around here."

"Joyce...yes, that's a good idea," said Teresa. "And, as far as what we're looking for...I don't exactly know. Just seems like a good place to go to search for clues."

"It probably is, dear, but are you prepared for the consequences?" asked Granger.

"Consequences?"

"Yes. Don't forget how the visions upset you. We're getting in pretty deep now, and you seem to be the one who's most affected by it all. Can you handle whatever may happen?"

"I've told you before that I think this is what I *have* to do. I can't pretend this is just another jar full of lightening bugs. It's not inconsequential as far as I'm concerned. Don't you understand that?" Teresa was emphatic.

"Well, I don't know about Granger," interjected Jack, "but I'm starting to. Why else would I have traveled so far? Why couldn't I just ignore those notes? None of this is logical, but I'm turning into a believer."

"Okay," said Granger. "If we all agree, then let's go ahead. But, let's keep going only as long as we're all still comfortable. If any one of us starts getting cold feet, we'll stop. Agreed?"

Both Teresa and Jack nodded in the affirmative, and they sat down at the table to finish breakfast.

Chapter Seven

In the searing heat of a blinding sun nearing its zenith, Teresa attempted both to collect her wits and to bridle her emotions, but no matter how much she tried, she couldn't stop thinking about Jack. She thought too about her upbringing as a good Catholic girl taught by habited nuns at a strict preparatory school. Sister Catherine would not be pleased with the fantasies that had raced through her mind on the front porch the previous night. Though she was no longer as faithful to her religious training as when she was young, Teresa was ashamed of herself. In her heart she wanted her marriage to last forever, and she resolved to conduct herself only in that manner. Sister Catherine would be so happy.

******

After a quick trip to the general store to talk to Joyce, they drove the few miles down the county road past the cemetery to the old Bollinger house.

"Funny. Even though I grew up here, I never knew the history of this house," confessed Granger. "This is the first time I've seen it up close."

"Wow. Feels like I'm in Gone with the Wind," said Teresa as they turned into the drive leading up to the white columned house that had been built in the 1840s. She glanced at both Granger and Jack and tried her best to imitate Scarlett O'Hara. "Fiddle-dee-dee. Which one of you is going to take me to the next cotillion ball?"

"I do declare, Miss Scarlett, I believe *I* will have that honor," said a smiling Granger as Rhett Butler.

Jack laughed. "I don't have enough southern blood in me to even *attempt* such an accent."

"You never know what we'll find out, Jack." She was Teresa again. "Sometimes we aren't who we think we are." Granger looked at her quizzically.

"We're here to see Mrs. Runyon. We called a few minutes ago," said Teresa to the graying servant who opened the heavy wood and glass front door.

"Oh yes, please wait in the parlor."

Teresa took a deep breath and drank it all in. They were directed to sit in a large, almost perfectly square room with fourteen-foot ceilings and a rustic but obviously refinished plank floor. Several Victorian-style couches and chairs, each paired with some variation of a classic mahogany occasional table, sat stiffly on black and gold area rugs around the room. A large brick fireplace with a carved oak mantel was the centerpiece on one wall, and wide divided light windows that were framed by elegant gold drapes stretched from floor to ceiling along the two exterior walls. Amazingly, sunlight seemed to stream into the room from every direction. Marveling at the scene before her, Teresa could almost visualize the room as it might have looked so long ago.

******

"Mother, Mother, look. Isn't it just delicious?" A young girl with long curly auburn hair ran into the room clutching her new blue satin dress.

Her mother, who was sitting in a chair near the brick fireplace, turned her head and smiled broadly as the she approached. "Why, yes, my dear. It's beautiful; it's truly beautiful. I'll tell Uncle Sibley how much you like his present."

"May I wear it to the party?"

"Well, I don't know. You may be a bit young."

"Oh, Mother. I'm eighteen now, way past marrying age. I think I'm ready, and Carrie thinks so too."

"Carrie? Since when do I listen to what Carrie says?"

"Now, Mother. She's more than just a servant. You said yourself she's going to be the first to get her freedom, soon as I'm out of the house."

"Yes, yes. I said that. Soon as I don't need her to help take care of you. It's what your father would've wanted. But, never you mind all that."

"Robert likes the dress, too, you know. He'd say I should wear it to the party."

"Should I call him in here now to confirm what you're saying?" Smiling devilishly, she replied, "Oh, no. No need. Take my word for it. He thinks I should."

Her mother smiled back knowingly. "I know your tricks, dear." She stared into the blazing fireplace for a moment and pulled her shawl more tightly around her. "Oh, all right. You can wear it. Tell Carrie to make sure it looks perfect."

"Thank you, Mother! You're wonderful. I love you." The girl squeezed her mother's hand and ran into the foyer carrying the blue dress. "Carrie! Carrie!" she yelled as she raced up the steps of the grand staircase.

******

"Granger."

"Huh?" Distracted, he was scanning his eyes around the room. "Wow, this is quite a place."

"Granger, I had another vision."

"Just now? But I couldn't tell."

"A young girl. I saw a young girl. I'm certain it was Sarah. She was carrying a new blue dress. She was asking her mother if she could wear it to a party. Her mother was sitting in a chair by the fireplace right here." Teresa pointed. "It was so real. It happened just that way. I know it."

"Now, calm down, honey." Granger touched her hand. It was cold and clammy, and her face was pale. "Do you want to go?"

"No, no. We need to go on." Her words were unconvincing because she herself was not convinced.

"Are you sure?" Jack instinctively reached out toward Teresa as well.

"I'm okay. I'm okay. It's gone now, but I'm as certain of what happened as I am of our being here today." Her eyes searched the room. "There's a lot here, a lot of feelings and emotions...things that happened a long time ago. I can sense it."

At that moment a tall stately woman in her forties walked into the room. "Good morning. I'm Phyllis Runyon. I was the one you talked to on the phone." She reached out her hand.

Granger offered his hand. "I'm Granger Walker, and this is my wife Teresa and a friend, Jack McAlester."

"Wonderful to meet you all. Please sit back down." She turned toward the foyer. "Charles, please bring us some coffee."

Teresa smiled at the bright, expressive face across from her. Marked by a large mouth with pristinely white teeth framed by bright red lips, the impeccably groomed woman had a regal look about her. If she had had really dark hair, her face could have been a model for a portrait on a Grecian urn. Brown eyebrows, manicured lashes, just a hint of eye shadow atop penetrating hazel eyes and a light brush of pink all accentuated her high cheekbones. Phyllis, in her light green dress, low heels and crystal jewelry, was much more formally attired than the three visitors. Teresa thought how well she fit the room, as if she could easily have lived here over a century ago.

"What can I do for you?" she asked.

"First, Mrs. Runyon, I'd like to thank you for letting us come by on such short notice," replied Teresa. "This is such a wonderful home, just gorgeous. Do you ever open it up for tours?"

"Why, thank you. We've really enjoyed restoring the old place. Not many of these dinosaurs left, you know. It's pretty authentic, except for some updating we did when we moved in about ten years ago. We'll probably have an open house at Christmastime this year—that is, if we can get it all together. And we're having a party this coming weekend. It's not exactly an open house, but quite a few people will be here." After a pause, she continued. "So...why have you come by today?"

As Charles served the coffee from an ornate silver pot, Granger said, "I don't know exactly how to put it, Mrs. Runyon, but we're here on an investigation."

"Investigation? Of what, Mr. Walker?"

"That's the part that's hard to explain. We think there was a murder."

Phyllis's eyes widened. "Murder? I don't understand."

"Actually, neither do we. By that I mean, the murder, we think, happened about a hundred fifty years ago."

Phyllis put down the steaming cup she was holding and stared at them incredulously. "I'm afraid I'm not following...."

Granger interrupted. "Well, we really don't know for sure, but we think a girl, Sarah Bollinger, who is buried in Balfour Cemetery, was murdered and the murderer was never identified. The thing is this crime happened in 1855—that is, if it happened at all."

A slight frown wrinkled Phyllis's forehead. "Well, I know that this girl was one of the Bollingers who once lived here in this house. But, other than that obvious coincidence, what does this whole thing have to do with me? And, if I might add, why are you investigating something that's, well, ancient history?"

"Again, these questions are difficult to answer." Granger glanced at Teresa and Jack. "For one thing, as you say, the girl was living in this house at the time of the murder. Also, my wife...." After he reviewed the events of the past couple of days and Jack revealed the notes he had received in San Francisco, Phyllis sat back hard against the cushion on the couch.

"Well, that's quite a story. I guess I'm not sure how to react."

"*That* we *do* understand," said Jack. "We haven't been sure how to react to all of this either. Obviously, the whole thing is like a light year or two beyond what one might accept as rational. But, one thing you must believe is that we're convinced there's something Teresa has tapped into. I'd be the last to accept all of this myself if I weren't directly involved, but my experiences over the past twenty-four hours have convinced me."

"Well, I suppose I believe that you all believe. I'm just having a bit of trouble with myself." Phyllis leaned forward, picked up the cup again and sipped her coffee. "For the moment, at least, let's assume you're correct about this...uh...murder. What can *I* do?"

"Uh...we don't know that exactly either, but we'd like to ask you a few questions and have the freedom to look around the place," said Granger.

"Yes, Mrs. Runyon," urged Teresa, "we'd appreciate your help and, I might add, your discretion."

"Discretion. I can buy that." She thought for a moment, and then replied, "Well, I've always liked mysteries. So, what is it you want to ask?"

"Well," said Jack, "I suppose the first question is whether you've ever uh...seen or heard anything in the house."

"You mean like a ghost or something?"

"Yes. A ghost or something."

"I can't say that I have. Of course, any house as old as this one always has a ghost story or two associated with it."

"What do you mean?"

"Just stories. You know, never confirmed. Sketchy stuff."

"Like what?" asked Teresa. "Please...please tell us." She leaned forward.

Phyllis sat back in her chair. "Well, the most repeated one is about a blue dress."

Teresa jumped, and Granger and Jack put down their cups.

Hesitantly, Teresa parroted, "Blue dress?"

"Yes. A blue dress rustling as a girl carries it up the stairs. I've heard that one several times, but I've never seen or heard anything myself."

"Bingo," said Teresa. A chill ran up her spine, and she touched Granger's hand. "The blue dress fits what I've seen. What else?"

"Oh, before we bought the place, the people who lived here at the time said they heard crying coming from one of the bedrooms upstairs, but...funny thing...they said it happened only once a year, during the winter, I think. You know...the usual sobbing, kind of the stereotype for all ghost stories."

"You've never heard any crying?"

"No. Nothing."

"This is really helpful. Disturbing, but helpful." Teresa sat back.

"Do you mind if we talk to anyone else who lives here, like your husband or children and maybe the servants?" asked Granger.

"Well, my husband George is in London until the end of the week. And, as for servants, there's only Charles and Gloria in the kitchen. Our kids are both grown now. They never lived here much, but they'll be at the party this weekend." She hesitated. "Why don't you all come to the party? You can talk to all of them then."

"Well, I don't know," said Teresa. For some reason she had a nagging fear, as if she were being drawn toward potential danger. She looked at Granger and arched her eyebrows.

Granger thought for a moment. "It'll be okay, dear," he assured her as he squeezed her hand. He turned back toward Phyllis. "Okay. Thanks for the invitation." He took a deep breath. "Well, this is more than we even hoped for. We really appreciate your help, Mrs. Runyon."

"Please, call me Phyllis."

Chapter Eight

"Hello Linda."

"Oh, are you on your way home?"

"No, I...I'm still in Houston. The meeting was delayed, so I'll have to stay another day or two."

"Another day or two? But what about the reception in Berkeley?"

"Uh...I'll have to see. I may have to stay here into the weekend."

"Umm."

"So, how are the kids?"

"They're fine."

Jack heard some voices in the background. "Who's that?"

"Oh, no one. Just some noise on the TV."

"Well, I have to run. Just wanted to let you know what's going on."

"Oh, okay...uh, I may be gone when you get back."

"Gone? Gone where?"

Linda hesitated. "Uh...to my mother's."

"Your mother's? You don't even get along with your mother."

"Yeah, well...she called. She asked me to come see her."

"But, what about the Berkeley thing?"

"Oh, I should be back by then. It'll be just a quick trip."

"I'll call you at your mother's place."

"Well...uh, I'll be pretty busy. I'll see you when you get back."

"Umm. I bet. Talk to you later."

Jack punched the button on his cell phone and thrust it roughly back into his pocket. Where could she *really* be going? A myriad of thoughts raced through his mind: she was leaving him, she was seeing another man, she was going on some clandestine shopping trip. Suddenly, he thought about Todd.

"Carol? It's me. I'm still in Houston. Lots of stuff going on, so I won't be in the office the rest of the week."

"But you have appointments. What do you want me to do?"

"Cancel everything. Tell them I'm...uh...indisposed or something."

"Jack, what's going on?"

"Just a meeting, and it's been delayed."

"I don't really believe you, but whatever you say goes. I'll cancel all your appointments, including the one with Mr. Johnson."

"Oh, yeah. Johnson. Uh, let me think." Jack had to have a good excuse for Mr. Johnson, the VP for Todd's biggest client, whose continuing good will was vital to the company. "Tell him there was a death in my family, and reschedule a meeting with him for next week."

"Jack! A death in your family? *Really*. You can do better than that."

"Well, tell him whatever you like. You'll have to deal with it because I've got to go."

"Okay, Jack. But, you're being very mysterious."

Jack realized the transparency of his alibis. He knew he needed to return to San Francisco quickly or at least he had to fabricate a more credible tale. In any case, it was not going to be easy to worm his way out of this one. Regardless of the risk, though, he had decided to stay in Balfour to see the mystery resolved. For some unfathomable reason, the events surrounding Sarah Bollinger's death had suddenly become more important than his career or even his marriage. He was being inexorably drawn to Teresa and, even more inexplicably, to the people whom neither he nor anyone alive today had ever known.

******

"Gloria, this is Mr. and Mrs. Walker and Mr. McAlester," said Phyllis. "They're visiting from out of town, and they have a few questions to ask you."

"Well, okay," replied Gloria hesitantly as they all sat down at the large table in the breakfast area.

"Now, before they start, I want you to know that whatever you say will be known only to us here today. No one else ever needs to know, and your answers won't affect your employment here."

"But, I always tell the truth." Gloria fingered her mousy brown hair and averted her eyes down toward the tabletop.

"I know, I know," assured Phyllis.

"What kind of questions are they going to ask?"

Phyllis suddenly realized that she might have made too much of the issue. "Never mind."

Granger quickly asked, "How long have you worked here, Gloria?"

"About three years."

"Are you here *every* day and night?"

"No, just Friday through Sunday and other days once in a while, when Mrs. Runyon needs me."

"And for how many hours on the days you're here?"

"From seven in the morning 'til six or seven in the evening, except longer when there's a special occasion."

"Have you ever spent the night?" he asked.

"Once or twice."

"Where did you sleep?"

"In the room off the kitchen." She pointed. "See. Through that door over there."

He glanced at Teresa. "Have you ever noticed anything unusual during any of the days or nights you've been in the house?"

"Unusual?"

"You know, like strange noises for instance?"

"Uh...no, not really."

Phyllis interrupted. "Now, remember. You can tell the truth. No one will repeat anything you say, and I can leave the room if you feel uncomfortable."

"No. That's okay. Well...." Gloria rubbed her forehead nervously and clutched her chin in her right hand.

"Well what? Your answer's really important," said Teresa.

"A couple of times I heard someone crying upstairs in the east bedroom."

"Crying?"

"Yes ma'am." Gloria raised her head and stared at an imaginary point across the room. "And not just crying...wailing almost, like they were in pain. It was really scary. I asked Charles to go upstairs to look around." Gloria shifted in her chair and rubbed the back of her neck.

Teresa pursued her story. "Did he?"

"Yes." Then she quickly added, "But he said he didn't find anything."

"Did *he* hear the crying?"

"He said 'no'."

"How long did the crying last and how often did you hear it?"

"Oh, I never thought about it, but, you know, it always lasted for maybe thirty minutes, then nothing. I only heard it a couple of times. In fact, it always happened in January. I remember 'cause it was so cold both times. One time we even had snow. We don't get snow very often."

"Umm...that would be right after Sarah's death," said Teresa.

"Huh?" asked Gloria.

"Never mind."

Granger picked up the questioning. "Now, Gloria, have you noticed anything else? Like, have you *see* anything strange?"

Gloria seemed energized now, as if she were suddenly enjoying herself. "One time, probably the first year I was here. Scared me so much I thought about leaving, but I needed the job."

"What happened?"

"I was upstairs helping Charles make one of the beds. Then, when I came out of the east bedroom I looked down the staircase, and I saw...uh...."

"What? What did you see?" asked Teresa.

"That is, I *thought* I saw a young girl carrying a blue dress. She was running up the stairs toward me. I was so shocked I just stood there. She was dressed real funny, in lots of petticoats, like in some old movie. And her hair was sort of reddish. I remember thinking how pretty she was."

"So...what happened then?" asked Granger.

"Well...I blinked a couple of times. I felt my heart pounding and I wanted to run, but I just couldn't move. I like froze where I was. Then, when she reached the top of the stairs, she disappeared, not ten feet in front of me."

"That's her," Teresa responded reflexively.

"Her? *Who*?" asked Gloria.

Ignoring her question, Teresa quickly pursued the story. "What else?"

"That's all. That's all I know. It's never happened again, I promise."

"Gloria, you never told me about any of these things," said Phyllis.

"Well, I thought you might say I was crazy, ma'am."

"No. I wouldn't think that. I just never knew anybody was hearing and seeing such things, at least since we moved in. Why haven't I ever seen or heard anything?"

"I don't know. Maybe you're just not receptive," replied Teresa.

"If I might interject," said Jack, "all this is pushing me way outside my comfort zone."

"Me too," admitted Granger. He looked at Teresa's smiling face. Teresa's doubt about her own sanity was fading and, for the first time in days, she was feeling relaxed again.

******

"This is the east bedroom," said Phyllis as she led Granger, Teresa and Jack on a tour of the house. "The room the crying came from."

Teresa walked over to the two large windows that looked out over the expansive yard. "Great view."

"Yes, it is, isn't it? The hills around here are just covered with wildflowers in the spring. It's one of the reasons we liked the house so much."

"Oh, and that four-poster bed. Looks like you'd need a ladder to climb into it at night."

"The furniture left in the house when we bought it was pretty much all Victorian."

A single mahogany nightstand next to the bed supported a simulated gaslight lamp, a large dresser with a beveled mirror sat against one wall, and a five-drawer chiffonier occupied another.

Looking back through the window, Teresa pointed across the fields. "What's that area over there?"

"Oh, that's the cemetery. See the arched gate entrance?"

"Uh...yes, yes...I see it." Teresa swallowed hard. She was certain that this was the bedroom she had seen in one of her visions. The table, the bed, the window—it was all the same. But she didn't know that the cemetery was so close that Vivian could see it from her bedroom day and night. She felt a pang of empathy and tears welled up in her eyes.

"Are the pieces in here original?" asked Jack.

"Well, we think so. Of course, we can never really be certain."

"Yes...you can be certain," offered Teresa, still transfixed by the view from the window.

"Huh? How's that?" asked Phyllis.

"Because I've seen it all before: the furniture, the window, all of it." She pulled a tissue out of her purse and wiped her eyes.

"Let's go on with the tour," interjected Granger. "I'd like to see the other bedroom."

The west bedroom was smaller, with only a single bed, a large trunk at the foot, a small dresser, and a large freestanding wardrobe with mirrors on the door.

"Some of the furniture was found in a tunnel that runs from the house to the building in back. I'll show it to you later."

Granger looked at the wardrobe. "We used to call these things 'chiffarobes'. I don't know if that's the proper name, though."

"What's this over here?" asked Jack. He was pointing at an intricately carved wooden box sitting on the nightstand.

"Now that's another mystery," said Phyllis. "It was in the…uh…'chiffarobe', way down in the bottom wrapped in some fabric and tied up with twine. Really strange."

"Why so?" asked Teresa.

"Well, it struck me at the time we found it that it must have been really important to whoever placed it there. It was so carefully wrapped up and secured."

"What was inside?" inquired Jack.

A wry smile crept across Phyllis's face. "Oh, just some old notes and letters."

Jack's eyes widened. "Notes…letters? Where are they now?"

"Why, they're still in there."

Jack slowly picked up the box, opened the lid carefully and pulled out a short stack of yellowed envelopes. They were letters all right. Suddenly his hand started shaking as he looked at the address:

Miss Sarah Bollinger
Balfour Plantation
Balfour, Texas

"Letters to Sarah Bollinger," said Jack.

"What? Letters?" Teresa rushed over to stare at the envelopes.

"I'm almost afraid to open them." His hands felt sweaty and his heart was pounding.

"Well, if you don't do it, I will," offered Teresa.

Jack took the letter at the top of the stack and pulled out the fragile sheet of paper inside.

Dear Sarah,
I will endeavor to come to see you, but the journey is long. Be patient, my dear.
Your obd serv^t,
Lance

"The date...what's the date?" Teresa was being impatient again.

"Uh...November 1, 1854," reported Jack.

"Hmm. November. Just a couple of months before her death," recalled Teresa.

"Pretty coincidental," said Granger.

"Coincidental? No, it's more than that," objected Teresa. "Almost a 'smoking gun', isn't it?"

"What do you mean?"

"This 'Lance'. He must have been the one."

"Who?"

"The one that the lady in my visions is talking about. You know, the gambler."

"Well, maybe."

"No 'maybe'. That's got to be it."

While Granger and Teresa were talking, Jack was rifling through the rest of the stack. He found what he was looking for at the bottom.

"Here's a letter that was never mailed."

"You mean a letter that Sarah wrote?" asked Teresa.

"Yes." Jack could barely hold the envelope when he saw the address.

Mr. Lance Feldcamp
Montgomery Street
San Francisco, California

"I...I can't believe it." Jack looked around for a chair. "I need to sit down."

"What do you mean?" asked Phyllis. "What is it you can't believe?"

Jack pulled one of the letters he had received from his back pocket. "My office is located on Montgomery Street. And look at this." He placed the two envelopes next to each other on the nightstand.

"Why, they're the same," said Phyllis.

"And look at the handwriting."

"The same."

Chapter Nine

They had had enough. After collecting some of the letters, the trio said their goodbyes to Phyllis but agreed to come back the next day to continue the tour. All of them were visibly shaken, and for an uncomfortable few minutes they sat quietly as Jack drove back along the county road past the cemetery.

Jack broke the silence. "How about a couple of stiff drinks and a good dinner? I have to mellow out a little." He was suddenly wishing he were at his favorite restaurant in North Beach. "You know, a carafe or two of good California wine might do wonders."

"That sounds good. Maybe you could recommend a vintage to us, since you're such an expert," said Granger.

"Yes...yes, *that* I could. It's one of the bennies of living in northern California."

Another army of summer storms was forming in the distance, and its vanguard of wind scattered leaves as they arrived at a small restaurant near the lake. A flash of lightning and a roll of thunder, like cannons firing behind the nearby hill, announced the arrival of the squall line. They quickly scurried into the front door just as the first large drops of rain began to fall.

"Ooh...we just made it," said Jack. "This time we didn't get drenched."

Granger looked around the restaurant. "Almost empty. Guess it's a bit early for a dinner crowd."

"How'd you know about this place?" asked Jack.

"Oh, it used to be *the* place to take a serious date. We couldn't come here very often—way too expensive for a high-schooler. So I've only been here a few times. This place used to have good catfish, all fresh from the lake, and their steaks weren't bad either. Been a long time since I ate here, though, so I'm not sure how good it is now."

"Pretty good," assessed Jack as he sipped the wine.

"Tastes good to me," Teresa chimed in.

"Yes," agreed Granger. "But of course I'm no connoisseur."

Teresa edged up next to Granger, but she couldn't conceal her interest in Jack. "Jack, tell us more about yourself. What about your family and your job?"

As the rain pounded the window, Jack talked slowly, careful not to reveal much more than they already knew: one wife, two children, one house, two cars and lots of work. He desperately wanted to be more open about the status of his marriage, but, for some reason, he couldn't. Jack knew Granger was waiting for him to say that he hadn't told Linda where he was, but he recoiled from serving up that tidbit to Teresa. In fact, he wished he had not let it slip to Granger. He needed time to weigh his options. Could Teresa be his savior, the key to a new life away from all of his troubles? She was obviously enamored. So, maybe all he needed to do was acquiesce...to just let it happen. Teresa stared trancelike at Jack as he talked, and Jack felt her eyes inspecting him. At once he felt uncomfortable and energized.

"How about you guys?" asked Jack as he sipped the fruity liquid from the rim of his glass.

"Well, we divide our time between here and Dallas, and we travel a bit." Under the unfamiliar influence of the wine, Granger rambled, "Yes, we always wanted children. We *did* have one child, but she died as an infant. It was an accident...eighteen years ago." He squirmed in his seat. "After we lost her, we went a long time before we tried again. Guess we waited *too* long." As he twirled the stem of his wine glass between his thumb and forefinger, he continued slowly. "So, I suppose it's our lot to go it alone."

"Granger, please," objected Teresa. "No more about that."

Jack interjected, "How about a toast?"

"A toast. Yes. What should it be?" asked Granger.

"Let's toast a new friendship: ours. How about that?"

Turning toward Jack and smiling, Teresa said, "Yes indeed. To our new friendship, across the miles and the many, many years."

Jack winked at her in a way that Granger couldn't see, and Teresa winced at this demeanor. Then they all pressed their glasses together with a soft clang.

"Good stuff," said Granger after he swallowed. "Jack, you chose well."

******

As they drove back to the house after a long dinner, they chatted and laughed about silly things. When he opened the car door at the house, Jack sniffed the sweetness in the air that had been washed clean by the rain.

"The air smells like fresh-washed sheets," commented Jack as he inhaled.

Though the storm persisted in the distance, the threat had now passed, and the slightly cooler atmosphere was filled with the usual night sounds. The only immediate evidence of the storm was the occasional drip of rainwater from the eaves and the squashing sound of their footfalls on the soggy grass as they walked to the back door.

"The wine's made me a bit sleepy," said Teresa, smiling. "Maybe it was just a little *too* good, Jack."

"Can't be *too* good. Take it from the connoisseur."

"Well, I'm pretty sleepy too. Think I'll take a shower and hit the hay," said Granger.

Jack thought for a moment. "I'm not quite ready for that. I probably need to call Linda before I turn in."

******

"Hi."

"Well, I was wondering if you were going to call again today," admonished Linda.

"Yeah. Uh, this is the first chance I've had this evening."

"More meetings, huh?"

"Yes. Meetings, meetings. You know how it is."

"I suppose. Uh…Jack, when you get back, we need to talk."

"Talk? About what?" He knew what was coming.

"Well, I probably shouldn't bring this up on the phone, but we need to talk about us…our relationship."

"What do you mean?"

"You know…how it's going, or *not* going."

Jack decided to fish around a bit. "You think there's a problem...I mean, more than the usual hassles?"

"Frankly, yes, I do. I feel a real tension between us. It's something we need to get out on the table."

He decided to be honest. "You're probably right. We need to air things out." Then, after a brief pause, "Linda, you've been taking too much out of our relationship lately and not giving enough."

"Well, for what it's worth, I feel the same way, only the other way around. Obviously we aren't going to solve this on the phone. Let's just plan to talk when you get home. By the way, when *will* you be back?"

"I already told you: maybe during the weekend. You're going to be gone to your mother's anyway, aren't you? I'm surprised you're not already gone."

"I'm leaving in the morning, and I should be back Friday. Juanita's coming over to stay with the kids."

"Well, I'll talk to you when I get back."

"Fine."

As he turned off the cell phone, Jack slumped in the chair and stared at the intricate patterns in the stippled ceiling. He felt limp. Maybe it was the wine or the conversation with Linda, but it really didn't matter. At least his marital problems were out in the open, and that, by itself, was a weight off his shoulders. He really *did* miss Linda's touch: her soft hands rubbing his back after a long day at work, her silken face against his when they kissed, her warm legs touching his under the covers at night. Deep down, he knew he would probably have to look elsewhere for those pleasures in the future. He also knew for a dead certainty: he *had* to have them, no matter what.

"Jack."

He jumped. "Huh?"

It was Teresa in that short robe again. "Jack, I was thinking...."

He looked into her glassy eyes. "Don't think, Teresa. Just go back to bed."

"I was thinking that you're holding back something...something about you and your wife."

"Why do you think that?"

"I feel it, Jack. I know. It's as if I've known you for a long time."

He twisted uncomfortably. "But what about Granger?"

"Granger's out completely. The wine really did him in. Now, what about it?"

"What?"

"You and your wife."

"Oh, that." He looked at Teresa and slumped again. "Yes, you're right. Linda and I...we...we're having some problems."

"What have you told her about what's going on here?"

"Not much." He felt as if he needed to confess. "Well, I mean, nothing really. She doesn't know where I am. She thinks I'm at some business meeting in Houston. I just couldn't tell her about all of this. She wouldn't understand, especially in light of our relationship issues."

"You poor thing." The wine had dissolved Teresa's inhibitions. Wedging herself into the chair, she put her arm around him. "You must be feeling pretty lonely right now."

"Uh...yeah. I guess I am."

As she started to rub Jack's shoulders gently, she asked, "Does this help?"

"Uh...yes, yes it does, but...."

"No buts, Jack. Just relax."

A myriad of confused, contradictory thoughts flashed through Jack's mind. Though he was thoroughly enjoying the experience, it was all happening so quickly, too quickly, and it was obvious that she her actions were being influenced by a wine-induced lack of control. It was too much for him to handle, especially with Granger no more than a wall away. He marshaled his resistance and suddenly stood up.

"Teresa. You have to get hold of yourself. Go back to bed. You and I are both tired tonight, and the wine was too much."

Teresa sat for a moment and, as if a switch had been tripped, said in a calm voice, "Yes, of course. You're right, Jack. I should go back to bed. I *am* tired." She stood up next to him. "Good night." Then she walked away and disappeared behind her bedroom door.

Jack was nonplused and numbed. He sat back down, thoughtless for some time. What should he do? He briefly considered leaving during the night and going back to San Francisco, but he rejected the idea. The mystery and the notes would remain to haunt him, and he remembered his resolve to see this thing to its end despite the risks. And what a risk he was running. Now he had to deal not only with Sarah but also with Teresa and his own indecision about his relationship with Linda. After what seemed like hours, he pulled himself out of the chair and went to bed.

Chapter Ten

Jack was up early the next morning poring over the letters they had taken with them. While he couldn't figure out all the details, he was able to piece together a time line of events that showed how the relationship between Sarah and Lance had developed.

"Morning," said Granger through a yawn as he staggered into the kitchen.

"Oh, good morning. Do you feel better now?" asked Jack as he looked up from the pile of letters strewn across the table.

"Well, at least I feel rested. Can't tell you whether I feel *better* yet." Granger struggled with a cup of coffee and sat down across from Jack. "Have you figured out anything from these letters?"

"Actually I have. It's quite a story. It'd probably make a good 1850's version of a modern soap opera. You know: May-September love, parental objections, surreptitious communications, secret meetings in New Orleans. Sarah's mother wanted to match her with one of the local young bucks, and she thought Lance was too worldly for her little girl."

"Kind of timeless, isn't it?"

"That's what I was just thinking. Nothing much changes over the years. Makes you feel closer to people who lived back then."

Granger picked up a couple of the letters and read them. "Boy, Sarah must've been really taken by this guy, but I see some deviousness in the way he writes to her."

"Yeah. I think her mother was right. This guy was some sort of rogue. He was much older than Sarah, so he'd probably been through quite a few women already. No telling."

"So, where are we on this?"

"I...."

Teresa walked up behind Jack. "Well, how's it going this morning?"

"Uh...okay," said Jack. He didn't quite know how to handle Teresa now. He didn't even know whether she would remember what had happened the night before. "How are you today?"

"Oh, fine. I was pretty looped last night. I don't remember much of anything after we got in the car."

"You don't?" asked Jack.

"Not much. I kind of recall sliding into bed, but that's about it. Everything else is a fog. I'm not used to having that much wine."

Reflexively Jack responded, "Well, that makes me feel better."

"How's that?" asked Teresa.

"Well, I mean, you acted kind of weird last night."

"Weird?"

"Oh, you acted like you didn't feel well."

"I guess I didn't, but I didn't know I didn't. Does that make sense?"

"Perfect sense," said Jack. Quickly changing the subject, he continued, "These letters are *very* interesting. I can piece together quite a story using them. Really helps me understand what was going on." He related the information he'd gleaned from the yellowed pieces of paper. "And one other thing: Did you notice the expression on Phyllis's face when we found the letters? I have a sneaking suspicion she knows more than she's admitting."

"I guess I was too shocked to notice at the time," said Teresa. "You know, it's all like a novel. One of these days, if we ever get out of this, Granger should write a book."

"Yeah, what a story," agreed Granger.

"Well," said Teresa, "I know we told Phyllis we'd be back at the house today, but I think we should try to talk to old Jed again."

"Jed? Why? You want to get shot?" asked Jack.

"I think he may know something, at least about the feud," explained Teresa. "He's our only known link...uh...*living* link, that is."

"Good point," said Granger. "And now that you know you're kin, maybe you two can...*relate*. Excuse the pun."

"Maybe I'll just hide behind the seat in the car," said Jack.

"There'll be no hiding. We're all in this together."

"All right, Granger, I'll go, but Teresa has to lead the way. He wouldn't dare hurt a woman...would he?"

"Don't bet on it. He's a crusty old cuss," said Granger. "I knew quite a few guys like him when I was growing up here. They jealously guard their view of the world, and they think that anyone with different ideas is crazy. Still and all, most of them are good people deep down. You just have to know how to approach them."

"Well, let's not waste a lot of time," advised Teresa. "I want to get back out to the house today too. That place is a treasure-trove."

****

Jed's old car had been moved. At least, thought Teresa, it was a sign that he had been out and about since they were there last.

"Well," said Jack as they parked in front of the trailer, "let's get this over with as soon as possible."

Teresa knocked on the door while the other two stood at the foot of the steps. "Mr. Feldcamp, I'm Teresa Walker. I...uh...we were here yesterday." She motioned briefly toward Granger and Jack and then turned back to face the rumpled, unshaven old man behind the screen.

Gruffly, "Yeah. I remember. Thought I told you I didn't want to talk."

"Yes, you did. But, since then, I've found out that you and I are related."

Now in a softer drawling voice, "Kin? You're kin to me? How d'ya know?"

"I have the birthmark, the circles. My father was Cecil Feldcamp, from Phoenix."

"You're Cecil's daughter?"

"You knew my father?"

"Good man, your dad. Uh...why don't y'all come in."

They filed into a cramped, cluttered space occupied by a short couch, two chairs, and a couple of end tables with lamps. A small desk filled one corner of the room, and off the kitchen a very narrow hall extended toward what appeared to be a bedroom. The place had obviously not been cleaned in a very long time. The carpet was worn and frayed, linoleum in the kitchen area was curled on the edges, and dirty dishes littered the tiny sink and spilled over onto the short counter. Heaps of papers, magazines and paperback books were stacked on every available space on the tables. Everything was dirty, and the odor was stifling.

"Have a seat," said Jed as he shoved a stack of old newspapers from the couch onto the floor. They all sat down gingerly.

"How's your father doing?" asked Jed.

"Oh, he passed away about four years ago," replied Teresa.

"Sorry to hear that. Like I said, he was a good man."

"How were you related to my dad?"

"First cousins. 'Course he was older, but I used to see him when I was a boy. I remember he had the bushiest hair."

"Well, he didn't have much left the last few years."

"Can't imagine. Used to be so thick."

"What about your mother?"

"She's gone too."

"Only met her once, when they got married. I was probably only about ten or eleven then. After that, I only heard in letters. I knew he had some kids. In fact, I think I got a couple of pictures of the whole family around here somewhere."

"I was the first. Then my brother Harris came along about four years later."

"Well, guess I can answer a question or two for old Cecil's daughter."

"Oh, yes, I *do* have questions." Teresa didn't want to reveal the *real* reason for their being there, so she had to be very careful. "Do you know anything about a feud between the Feldcamp family and a family named Bollinger who used to live around here? I confess I never heard anything about it growing up in Arizona."

"The feud. Oh, that. Well, I don't know much."

"Tell us what you can," said Granger.

"All I know is it all started a very long time ago. Seems one of the Bollingers, a young girl, was murdered by a Feldcamp. This Bollinger girl—she's buried out in the cemetery down the road here. My mother used to say the Bollingers would go out there at least once a year to visit her grave. Everybody thought they were all crazy...probably they were."

"Who murdered her?" asked Teresa.

"Well, they said it was a Feldcamp, but they never could prove it. They claimed it happened after a party, a real gruesome murder. The Bollinger girl and the murderer were in love, but it all went wrong somehow and he killed her. At least, that's what they said."

"Why was it so gruesome?"

"Don't really know. People just used to say she was all chopped up. You know, with some sort of knife."

"What was the Feldcamp guy's name?"

"Don't know that either." Suddenly he smiled and chuckled. "Guess I'm the only Feldcamp left here now." He paused for a moment and squinted his eyes. "You know, I just thought of something. We Feldcamps outlasted the Bollingers."

"Huh?"

"Now they're all gone and we're still here. Kind of funny." He chuckled again.

Teresa stole a glance at the incredulous expressions on Granger's and Jack's face. "Can you tell us anything else?"

"That's all. It happened so long ago. This is the first time I've talked to anybody about it since I was a teenager, I think. Even then the whole thing was sort of like a legend. You know—old and maybe not even true."

"Well, you've been very helpful," interjected Granger.

"Why in hell would y'all be asking about something like this?" asked Jed in his ugly voice. "You gonna get one of those crazy sensation magazines to do a story about it?"

Teresa had to think fast. "No, no. I...I'm doing some genealogical research on the family. This has human interest written all over it, even though it's kind of gruesome."

"Yeah, but it might not even be the truth," offered Jed.

"I know, but a lot of family histories include stuff like this. It's so intriguing it shouldn't be lost. I mean, you may be the only one left who knows anything about it."

"Maybe."

"Well, we don't want to take any more of your time," said Teresa.

"Yes. Again, thanks for your help," added Jack as he reached for the door. He clearly wanted to leave as soon as possible.

"Uh...don't mention it," replied Jed. Then, looking at Teresa, he added in a much softer voice, "I enjoyed talking to you. You know, you have a lot of hair like your dad."

As they drove away, Teresa looked back. "I kind of feel sorry for old Jed."

"How's that?" asked Granger.

"Well, he's lonely. All he does is sit around that trailer day in and day out. And, after all, we *are* family."

"You know, the whole time we were sitting there in that mess, I was having a really hard time believing you're related to that guy. You and he are so different, yet your dad and his dad were brothers," said Jack.

"Different circumstances yield different results," answered Teresa.

"I guess. Life is strange."

"You think he was telling us the truth?" asked Granger.

Teresa quickly answered, "Oh, I think so. In fact, I know so. I have a feeling about Jed, and remember: I'm the clairvoyant one around here. You boys have to trust me on this one."

Chapter Eleven

The sun was just past high noon when Phyllis greeted them at the front door.

"I think I'll take you down into the basement and show you the tunnel we were talking about yesterday," said Phyllis.

They followed her to a short door behind the grand staircase and stood at the top of a narrow set of steps. Below them lay ink-black darkness. Phyllis turned on a flashlight and reached for a lantern hanging nearby. Curtains of cobwebs dangled from the rough-hewn beams overhead, clouds of fine dust floated in the air, and the strong musty odor of warm stagnant air enveloped them. Steadying themselves with the rope railing, they carefully navigated the fifteen steps to the basement floor.

"Here. Someone can use the lantern," instructed Phyllis.

"Ugh. This is allergy city," said Teresa as she reached the base of the creaking stairs. "What's down here anyway?"

"You mean other than spiders and rats?" joked Granger.

Teresa cringed. "I'll pretend you didn't say that. I'm asking Phyllis, and I meant what *other* things."

"Actually, we haven't finished going through everything yet. Mostly it's broken pieces of furniture, discarded toys and boxes of old newspapers, some dating back a hundred years or more. You can see everything's a real mess. I know we need to get rid of most of it, but 'out of sight, out of mind' as they say. Oh, and there are several trunks, still locked I'm afraid."

Jack waved the lantern in several directions trying to determine the size of the basement. "How big *is* this thing?"

"Oh, it extends under the whole house. We've never really explored all of it. The place is so full that I think you'd have to remove some of the stuff to reach the other end."

******

Vivian yelled from the top of the stairs. "Robert! Robert! Where are you?"

"Over here, Mother."

She lit a candle and carried it in the direction of the voice. "What are you doing?"

"Just storing some things away, as you asked me to do."

She still couldn't locate him. "Robert, please! I'm frightened down here. Where *are* you?"

Robert came up from behind and touched her. "Eek!" Vivian turned around and raised her hands up toward her face. "Robert!" she shouted. "You scared me. I almost dropped the candle." After taking a couple of breaths, she continued, "Now come on back upstairs."

"But I'm not finished down here."

"You can finish your work later. I need you upstairs."

"All right. I'll be there directly. You go on back."

Vivian turned toward the stairs and yelled, "Carrie! Come help me back up the steps."

Robert returned to his task of filling a trunk. He quickly closed the lid and locked it. Meanwhile, Carrie helped Vivian up the narrow stairs and through the small door above. As he climbed the stairs, Robert wedged the trunk key into a small crevice between the support beams, blew out his candle, and stepped through the small opening.

******

"Guys, I just had another flash," reported Teresa.

"A flash? You mean another one of your visions?" asked Granger.

"Yes." Teresa instinctively reached out for Granger again, and he took her hand. It was cold and clammy. "But it's over now."

"You mean you saw something?" asked Phyllis.

"Something that happened down here. I think it was after Sarah's death. Robert was storing some things away in a trunk, and Vivian came down to get him to go back upstairs."

"What was he putting in the trunk?" asked Jack.

"I couldn't tell. Looked like stacks of fabric or drapes or something like that. But I did see one thing for sure."

"What?" asked Granger.

"Well, after he locked the trunk, he hid the key, and I saw where he put it."

Phyllis felt her heart racing. "Where?"

"Between some wallboards near the top of the steps. Up there." Teresa pointed toward the small door through which they had just passed.

"Hmm...well, let's put your clairvoyance to the test," said Jack.

While the other three waited on the basement floor, Jack climbed back up thirteen of the fifteen steps and touched the wall next to the stairs. "Here?"

"Not quite. To your right a bit," instructed Teresa.

"Here?"

"Yes. There somewhere."

Jack ran his hand across the brick and mortar that formed the foundation of the old house. He found mounds of dried-up mud, probably made by dirt daubers, layers of cobwebs built up over a century or more, and one ancient book of matches.

"Aha!"

"What?" exclaimed Teresa. "You find it?"

"No. I found a box of matches."

"What?"

"A box of matches." He shook the box, slid it open and struck one. "Amazing. Still good." He examined it carefully and chuckled. "There's a biplane on the front. Guess that dates it a bit."

"What else?"

"Lots of spidery stuff...uh...wait. Here's something else." His hand had hit a piece of metal, long and slender but flared at both ends. "Well, I'll be."

"Tell us what's going on," Teresa called out as she felt a chill.

"It's a key, an old key—just like you said." Jack held up the rusting piece in his hand and tried to illuminate it with the lantern. "You probably can't see it very well from down there, but, by golly, Teresa got it right."

Phyllis's eyes widened as she turned toward Teresa. "Well, I guess that builds your credibility."

"I guess," Teresa said. She wasn't sure whether she should be happy or frightened or maybe a bit of both, but she felt the contentment of having proved her sanity yet again.

"Well, bring it down here," ordered Granger. "Let's *all* have a look."

Each of them inspected the key in the fickle glow of the flashlight and lantern.

"Wonder what it belongs to," said Jack.

"Why, the trunk, of course," replied Teresa. "Only, where's the trunk?"

"We've found a bunch of trunks down here," said Phyllis. "And there may be even more in the parts of the basement we've never been in." She waved the light beam into the seemingly endless black ahead of them. Heaps of boxes and remnants of old furniture blocked the way.

"It'd take a lot of work to move all this stuff out of the way and search the whole basement," said Granger.

"Yes. But maybe we might be lucky and find it right away," said Teresa.

"Perhaps," admitted Phyllis. "If we don't find a lock the key fits among the trunks we can get to, then we can always consider other alternatives."

"Or just give up," said Jack.

"No. We can't just give up," Teresa objected.

"But we don't even know if this key or the trunk or whatever is in it is significant."

"Right. But it *could* be. I mean, the fact that I...uh...*saw* it all happen implies it's important."

"So you're getting selective visions now?" asked Jack.

Frustrated, Teresa barked her reply. "I'm getting them for a reason, and they aren't just random."

"Okay, okay. I suppose if we admit the visions are real, we also have to buy into some sort of intelligence behind them," said Phyllis. "I'm on Teresa's side of this argument."

"I'm on Teresa's side of *every* argument," said Granger as he put his arm around his wife.

"Thanks, dear, but I'm not sure that's true."

"Maybe not, but it's true in this case."

"Well, let's table this exchange for later and go on to the tunnel," said Phyllis.

"Yes. Let's," agreed Teresa.

Phyllis led them along a very narrow path that had been cleared through the disorganized piles of discarded items. They saw an old bicycle with a large front and a much smaller back wheel, several decapitated dolls in various stages of undress, and a rack of dresses in the style of the twenties and thirties. Old hats, including what appeared to be a World War I doughboy helmet, still clung to one of several costumers.

"What a place," exclaimed Granger. "I bet some antique dealer would like to rifle through this stuff. Could be some gems in here."

Phyllis agreed, "No telling what we'd find if we ever took the time to clean it out." Suddenly, they reached what appeared to be a dead end. "Here. Here's the entrance to the tunnel." She tried to push a large wooden panel leaning on the foundation wall.

"Let us help you with that," said Granger. He and Jack grunted as they leaned against the heavy piece of oak and moved it out of the way.

Phyllis waved the focused beam from her flashlight down the corridor that was now open to them. "This is it. It's really narrow and has kind of a low ceiling. It runs from here to a small room beneath one of the outbuildings. When we moved in the whole thing was crammed with stuff, mostly furniture. A few of the items in the small west bedroom were found in here. We still haven't cleaned everything out."

"How'd you know that's where the pieces should go?" asked Teresa.

"We didn't, but the style seemed to fit, and some of the pieces, including that chiffarobe, as you call it, were marked on the bottom with the words 'west b'. We figured that might mean west bedroom."

"Makes sense to me," said Jack.

"We wouldn't have moved anything out if we hadn't been so intrigued by the tunnel. I've always wondered what they used it for."

Granger, ever the history student, spoke up. "Well, I know some tunnels were dug as hiding places in case the Yankees ever invaded, and some tunnels were a way of escape for slaves. I guess we'll never know about this one. In the end it just became a large underground closet."

They walked through the tunnel to the small room at the other end. On the way, Granger noticed a pile of the biplane matchboxes stacked in one corner of the room. The sunlight blinded them as they reached the top of the ladder and opened the trap door built into the wood floor of the outbuilding.

"Ugh. You don't realize how bright the sun is until you've lived with the moles for a while," said Granger as he squinted his eyes.

Teresa dusted her off her clothes. "I feel grimy and sweaty."

"Ladies don't sweat, my dear, men do. Ladies merely perspire," scolded Granger mockingly.

"Well, this lady is perspiring *big time*," said Teresa.

As she was cleaning herself off, Phyllis suddenly raised her arms. "Tell you what. Why don't you all go clean up and come back here for dinner tonight. I'll ask Gloria and Charles to stay late, and we can use the good dishes in the formal dining room. We almost never have occasion to do that."

"But, what about the key? And are you sure you want to go to all that trouble?" asked Teresa.

"The key will wait. If there's a trunk the key fits, it's been there for a hundred fifty years…so, what's one more day? Besides, having dinner here tonight would be fun. It'd give us a chance to talk in somewhat more, should I say, *pleasant* circumstances. What do you say?"

Teresa stared at Granger to look for approval in his eyes. "Uh…okay. What about it, guys?"

"I like the idea. We have to eat anyway," replied Jack.

"Me too," responded Granger. He thought for a moment and quickly added, "You know, I sometimes participate in Civil War reenactments. So, should I show up in my uniform? We could make it a kind of a costume event."

"If you so desire, sir, I would be honored," said Phyllis in an obviously exaggerated drawl.

"Since I'm from California, maybe I should come as a Yankee," offered Jack. "But I don't know where I'd find an outfit like that around here."

"I have one you could fit into," said Granger. Then, chuckling, he said, "I never know which side I might have to be on during one of those reenactments."

Uncharacteristically, Phyllis almost giggled out loud. "Well, I guess we're all set. See you all later."

Chapter Twelve

The house was particularly resplendent when they returned about half past seven. The lights in all of the front rooms were on, as were the four ponderous lamps hanging by massive chains from the ceiling of the second-floor veranda, and torches flared along the brick drive leading up to the front porch. Streaming rays from the setting sun that fell broadly across the newly mowed lawn created long shadows of the pines and pecan trees. The color of the grass was almost blindingly green, and the huge magnolia trees at the base of the brick walkway were in full bloom.

"Wow. The old place looks fantastic. Right out of a fairy tale," said Teresa as they walked up the steps of the columned porch. "The air smells like rain and fresh grass, so clean and sweet." She inspected Granger and Jack. "You guys look great too." She looked at Granger, batted her eyelids and adjusted his tie. "I love a man in uniform. I feel like I should be dressed in a hoop skirt."

Jack was obviously uncomfortable. He pulled at the collar around his neck and fumbled with the buttons on his long dark blue coat. "I don't think this thing fits me the way it's supposed to. And how in hell did those guys stand these uniforms in this heat?"

"I know it's not quite right, but you'll get used to it," said Granger, who looked very much at ease in his custom-tailored reproduction of a Confederate officer in Hood's Texas Brigade. Fully equipped with gold braids and gloves, it fit him perfectly. He was even wearing his great-great grandfather's old watch and fob. "Only thing is I didn't have time to grow my usual beard," he muttered to Teresa as Charles opened the door.

"Why, you boys look like you just stepped out of a history book. I hope there'll be no hostilities tonight," exclaimed Phyllis when she met them in the foyer. "You look nice too, Teresa."

Almost apologetically, Teresa replied, "Well, I didn't have a real period costume."

"Neither did I, but our more modern outfits will have to do."

"Drinks will be served in the parlor," said Charles. He was decked out in a bow tie and long coat. They briefly caught a glimpse of Gloria, similarly formal in attire, as she prepared the dining room table.

"Boy, you went all out tonight. What's with Charles and Gloria?" asked Teresa. "Charles really looks like an English butler in those clothes."

"Well, I thought I wouldn't hold anything back," replied Phyllis. "Dressing up like this occasionally is fun, and it's practice for the big party this weekend."

"Yeah," agreed Teresa as they walked into the brightly lit room. She cupped her hand and whispered so that only Phyllis could hear. "I don't think the guys, especially Jack, are as happy about this as we are. Besides, they had to dress in the heat. Our air conditioner went out this afternoon."

Phyllis muffled a giggle. "Oh no. I know it's not funny, but you all must have been in meltdown."

"What was that?" asked Granger.

"I hope you like champagne," Phyllis said quickly.

"Champagne? Oh, I love it, and I can't remember the last time I had some," said Teresa.

"California champagne?" asked Jack. "I think it's the best, but you know I'm prejudiced."

"It's California champagne, but let me warn you that the wine with dinner is from Texas. You know, we have a wine industry out in the Hill Country and in West Texas."

"I've heard about it, but I confess I've never tried any. Guess this is as good a time as any."

As they sipped tall glasses of champagne, Phyllis spoke up. "I...I hesitate to mention this tonight when we're trying to have some fun, but something happened after you all left today."

"Something to do with our mystery?" asked Teresa.

"Maybe. I'm not sure. I had talked to Charles and Gloria about staying late this evening, and I was here in the parlor when I heard some strange noises coming from the basement. So, I opened the door behind the staircase and flashed a light down the steps. I couldn't see a thing, and I was afraid to go down there by myself to check. Then I yelled 'Is anyone there?'. After a few seconds I heard what sounded like someone running away in the direction of the tunnel. In fact, there was a crash, as if something in the basement had been knocked over...then nothing. No one came out through the door, so whoever it was is either still there or they exited through the tunnel and the outbuilding."

"You think someone got in through the tunnel and was just looking around?"

"No. We keep that building locked. And, as far as I know, only my family and you three know about the tunnel anyway. Now here's the really strange part. Later, when I was in the kitchen, I noticed that the backside of Charles's pants had a bit of dust and cobwebs on it."

"Charles? Did you ask him about it?"

"Yes. He said he'd been out in the garage and probably rubbed up against something."

"You believe him?" asked Teresa.

"I don't know...I suppose I do. He's worked for me for over ten years, and I've never had a reason to doubt him in the past. But it's a strange coincidence."

"Is there any reason he'd need to go down into the basement?"

"I can't think of any. But, in any case, why would he have lied about it? I mean, if he had a good reason to be there, then he shouldn't have been afraid to tell me."

"You're right," said Granger. He thought for a moment, looked around the room, and continued, "Let me try something. Maybe we can figure out whether he was the culprit."

"How can you do that?" asked Phyllis.

"Just follow my lead when he comes in next time," replied Granger.

A few minutes later, Charles brought another bottle of champagne. As he was topping off the glasses, Granger spoke up. "Uh, Charles, Mrs. Runyon wants the candles on the mantle lit. You know, to enhance the atmosphere in here. So, do you mind lighting them?"

"Do you have a cigarette lighter or some matches, sir?" asked Charles.

"Actually, I don't. No one smokes these days."

Charles fumbled nervously as he searched the drawers of the end tables. Playing along, Phyllis urged him on. "Charles, don't you have some matches somewhere? You always seem to be prepared."

Clearly flustered, he sputtered, "Uh...yes ma'am. I...I know I have some matches around here. Umm." He patted his pants and reached into one after another of his jacket pockets. Suddenly, a smile grew across his face. Something rattled. "Ah, yes. I found some. Knew I had them." As Charles lit the five candles on the mantle, Granger secretly made sure the others noticed the cover of the box Charles had retrieved.

After Charles left the room, Granger said, "Remember the matchbox with the biplane on it in the basement? Well, there was a whole pile of matchboxes like that in the little room at the end of the tunnel. That's where Charles must have gotten his. He *had* to have been down there in the tunnel."

"Good sleuthing," said Jack.

"Well done, dear," agreed Teresa. "How did you know he'd have one of those match boxes?"

"I didn't. Just took a risk."

"And you remembered about the pile of matchboxes in the tunnel."

"Well, it was a little thing, but you never know what might be important. You know, some things are really consequential."

"You mean like lightning bugs?" asked Teresa.

Phyllis tilted her head, frowned and looked at Teresa. "What do lightning bugs have to do with it?"

"Oh, nothing," said Teresa.

"It's some sort of inside joke," said Jack quickly to Phyllis. "They wouldn't explain it to me either."

Phyllis was analytical. "Well, in any case, now we know it was Charles that I heard in the basement. He has knowledge of the tunnel, and he didn't want me to know he was down there. Now why would that be?"

"Phyllis, what do you really know about Charles? What's his last name?" asked Granger.

"His name is Breck, Charles Breck. As I said before, he's worked here for more than ten years. He's been an excellent, loyal employee. He's a Balfour native, but all of his family is dead or they've moved away. He seldom takes days off, even holidays. He's never been married, and he's a loner." She rubbed her hand down one of her cheeks.

"In fact, I can't recall the last time he mentioned doing anything with a friend."

"Where does he live?"

"Near the lake. I've been to his place once. Several years ago when he was sick I took some food over to him. It's a small house I think he inherited from his parents."

"Well, he sounds okay. Any previous trouble with the law?" asked Granger.

"Oh no...none at all," said Phyllis. "I wouldn't have someone with a record working here, especially since I'm alone so much."

Teresa had a nagging feeling that this was an important piece of information that was somehow linked to the mystery. But, despite all her clairvoyant powers, she didn't have any idea of the connection.

"At this point, I guess it's just another mystery," mused Teresa. "I think the answers will all be revealed...in time, that is. Until they do, let's try to forget all this crazy stuff for a few hours. I'm on overload right now."

"I agree with Teresa," said Jack as he held up his champagne glass and pulled again at his collar. "Since we're already all dressed up, let's not fritter away precious social time."

Phyllis chimed in, "You're right, Jack. I think dinner is ready anyway."

Granger stood up, bowed deeply and drawled, "I'd be honored, ladies, if you'd accompany this soldier of the South to our evening repast..." Then, glancing at Jack, he added, "...under a flag of truce, of course."

Not to be outdone, Jack leaped to his feet at the other end of the couch, bowed and said with decorum, "As a representative of the Grand Army of the Republic, I heartily agree, but I insist that I serve as an escort as well."

As they walked to the dining room, Granger with Teresa on his arm and Jack with Phyllis, Granger turned to Jack. "Good job, Billy Yank."

"Good job, Johnny Reb," Jack replied.

******

They sat around the long rectangular table covered with cream-colored linen and crowned by greenery and magnolia blooms. With the electric lights dimmed, scarlet candles along the center of the table glimmered softly, warming the cool yellow wallpaper and throwing flickering shadows across the faces of everyone at the table.

"Everything is just beautiful, Phyllis," effused Teresa. "The china, the silver, the food. And these crystal glasses: Where did you get them?"

"Oh, they're family heirlooms. You know, the ones no one ever actually uses."

"The wine's great too," admitted Jack as he set his glass back down on the table.

"Thanks. You know, people in the rest of the world think all we have in Texas is dust and oil. While we admit to having more than our fair share of both, we sometimes feel stereotyped. Now you can testify from personal experience that we have far more."

Smiling broadly, Jack responded, "Yep. Much, much more."

Jack was enjoying himself immensely. The letters, the mystery, Linda, and his career—all his troubles—faded in the magical glow of the evening, and he was caught up in it all. He looked at the others seated around the table and thought how they had been strangers only a few days ago but, since then, by chance, or perhaps by design, he had been drawn into their lives. They were all warm and genuine, and, unlike those who populated his life in California, they demanded neither his time nor his money. He felt almost drugged by this new experience and, particularly, by Teresa. He marveled at her winsome smile, at the smoothness of her lightly tanned skin and at her engaging personality. He was uncontrollably drawn to her...entranced, bewitched. He was having trouble keeping in mind that the evening and all its associated emotions were, like the aura of the uniform he was wearing, merely fantasies.

"Now we're going to have what I would call the pièce de résistance," announced Phyllis as the main course was removed from the table. She motioned to Gloria, who was standing in the door leading to the kitchen.

"I wonder what it is," mused Teresa.

"Probably some fancy French dish," said Granger.

"Or maybe something uniquely Texan," speculated Jack.

"Well, Jack, you're closer to being right." Phyllis removed the cover to reveal a magnificent banana pudding topped with lightly browned meringue. "I hope everyone likes bananas."

Exclamations of endorsement went around the table as they tasted the sweet dessert and sipped on steaming cups of dark-roast coffee.

"What a meal," exclaimed Jack after they finished and sat back in their chairs.

"Yeah. Great stuff. I don't think I've had such a good home-cooked meal since my mother used to make dinners for me over thirty years ago," said Granger. He quickly glanced at a frowning Teresa. "Uh...with several notable exceptions, that is."

"Umm...don't say that just because you want to stay out of trouble," advised Teresa.

"Maybe I better just keep my mouth shut," said Granger. "I can't go wrong that way."

Everyone laughed.

******

Later, back in the parlor over after-dinner drinks, Jack waxed philosophical. "You know, if it hadn't been for the mystery, we all wouldn't be here together tonight, and we wouldn't have had such a good meal."

"Well, you're right about that," admitted Teresa.

"And, I might add, Granger and I wouldn't be dressed in these uniforms. Makes me appreciate those Civil War re-enactors like you, Granger."

"You know, my unreconstructed grandfather objected to the term 'Civil War'. He used to say there wasn't anything 'civil' about it. He insisted on the more Confederate-friendly name for it: 'The War Between the States'. Now I've gotten so used to saying 'Civil War', I don't think about it anymore, and, to rationalize, I sort of turn my grandfather's objection around. I say enough time has past since it happened that now we *can* be 'civil' about it."

"Enough history. You focus too much on what happened in the past, dear," said Teresa. As soon as the words left her mouth, she knew she shouldn't have said anything.

Granger glared at her. "Well, the evening had been going pretty well until you brought that up."

Jack and Phyllis looked at each other and frowned.

"Well, anyway, we need some good thinking about our current problem, so let's focus on that right now," said Teresa quickly.

Jack shrugged his shoulders. "Yeah, well...I confess I'm stumped."

"I admit it's confusing, but we do have some facts," said Granger. "We just need to follow our leads, especially this thing about Charles. Somehow I think he's connected to the murder."

"So, now we really think this girl...Sarah...was murdered?" asked Phyllis.

Granger answered, "What else could've happened? I guess we have to admit that Teresa is seeing some sort of visions, that they're not figments of her imagination and that, in fact, other people besides Teresa have heard and seen things. Right?"

"Yep," said Phyllis.

Jack nodded his head in agreement.

"The question is whether Charles is involved," said Teresa.

"I don't think there's any doubt about it," said Granger. "He must've overheard our discussions about Sarah, and he knew we went down into the basement earlier today. I think he was trying to figure out what we'd found, or maybe he was looking for a key too."

"You mean he knows about the trunk?" asked Teresa.

"Maybe. Or he may not know about *the* trunk, just that there are several trunks down there that are locked and he wants to go through them."

"Too many possibilities," said Jack. "We have to narrow them down. Why don't we try to find out more about Charles's background? Phyllis, you said he's a Balfour native. There must be some birth records on him at the county seat. At least that would be a start."

"That's a good idea," said Phyllis. "Say, I'm starting to feel like Dr. Watson."

"Well, I'll let you know when I start believing I'm Sherlock Holmes," joked Teresa.

"What about the key? How do we find which trunk it fits?" asked Jack.

"As Teresa and I said, we can try using the key on the two or three trunks that are easy to get to," said Phyllis. "Maybe we'll be lucky."

"Good. Let's do that," said Granger. "That's probably all we can plan for right now, and it's a good start."

"Yeah," said Teresa. "I guess we need to get back to our hot house." She stood up as if she were ready to leave.

"Listen," said Phyllis. "I know this is spur of the moment, but why don't you all just stay here tonight. It's late, and you don't have any air conditioning anyway. You wouldn't get much sleep if you went back to your place, and you need to be rested tomorrow. How about it?"

"Well, I don't know," said Teresa. She wasn't eager to spend the night in the old house because she felt the latent energy in the rooms. At the same time, she knew that any event, however unpleasant, could speed their understanding of the mystery.

"I'm for it," said Jack. "I wasn't looking forward to sleeping in the heat."

"Neither was I," agreed Granger. "If you're willing to stay, dear, I am." He took Teresa's hand and squeezed it. "I'll be right beside you all night."

Teresa thought for a moment. "I guess I have to be brave. I couldn't live with myself if I didn't face this thing. After all, what's the worst that could happen?"

"I don't want to answer that," said Granger. "Let's just do it."

Teresa shrugged. "All right. We'll stay."

"Great," said Phyllis. "I have some night clothes you all can borrow. And you won't have to sleep in the two bedrooms in the old part of the house. You can take rooms in the new wing. It's much more modern, and it doesn't have all the historical baggage the old rooms do."

"Sounds good," said Jack. "I'll register for the night. Where do I sign in?"

"No guest registration necessary," replied Phyllis. "Just follow me."

They all smiled at one another and followed Phyllis up the stairs.

Chapter Thirteen

Phyllis led the trio past the old east and west bedrooms and into the new part of the house, where the décor was decidedly more modern.

She took Granger and Teresa to one suite and Jack to another. "Might as well use the good bedrooms tonight," she said to Teresa as she opened the door. "We had this bedroom and bath and the one next door built just before we moved in, and the other two bedrooms without baths were added then too. George and I have our master bedroom downstairs." As they looked around the room, she added, "Don't be frightened by all the stuff in here. These rooms used to be inhabited by teenagers. Sometimes they can be even scarier than malevolent spirits."

Teresa examined the posters plastered over almost every square inch of the walls. "I see what you mean."

"These are two *more* rooms we need to clean out," added Phyllis. She thought for a moment and chuckled. "Maybe I should get the kids to help me when they're here this weekend."

"This'll be very comfortable," said Granger as he patted the soft bedspread.

In the room next door, Jack was equally grateful for being offered a cool room for the night. "All I need is a good mattress. I've already checked out this one, and it'll do fine. Thanks a lot for letting us stay, Phyllis."

"You're welcome. If you need anything, just knock on my door. Gloria and Charles will be in at seven, and breakfast will be ready in the dining room by seven thirty. Hope you sleep well." With that, she left him to go to her bedroom downstairs.

"Guess I forgot what it's like to be around teenagers," said Teresa as she was undressing.

Granger was philosophical. "Well, it doesn't take long to be looking back at them across a gaping generation gap. I think we've been past all that for more than thirty years."

"Yeah," said Teresa as her lips curved into a smile, "but I wouldn't go back to being a teenager. I couldn't handle it. I'm quite happy where I am right now." She walked over to Granger, untied his gold sash and started unbuttoning his shirt. "Like I said earlier, I just can't resist a uniform."

Granger grinned back at her as he saw the twinkle in her eyes. Then, in character, he drawled, "Now, Ma'am, you're not bein' very lady-like. As an officer, I'm duty-bound to make sure you don't lead my men astray."

"Well, colonel," Teresa replied as she continued to undress him, "maybe you could best do your duty by taking care of me yourself." With that, they fell onto the bed in each other's arms and finished undressing.

******

Next door, Jack was tired. He took off his clothes in the dim light of the small ginger jar lamp on his nightstand and, for a while, sat limply on the side of the bed. As he lay across the bed and stared at the ceiling fan rotating slowly above him, he could hear one of those whippoorwills again, it's lonely call echoing through the trees—loud, then soft, close, then far away. Was it really an echo or were there two whippoorwills? He drifted to sleep gently, floating away weightlessly while he listened to that solitary song coming from out there, somewhere in the inscrutable darkness.

******

"Robert, I found a letter from that man," said Vivian as she fumbled with the papers on her desk. "Sarah has been corresponding with him. I know all about it."

Robert knew what Vivian meant, but he feigned ignorance. "A letter? A letter from whom?"

"From that Feldcamp person who lives in San Francisco, the one she met the last time we were in New Orleans. Apparently, she's asked him to come see her here when we have the party next month."

"From California? She wants him to come all the way back here? It's such a long trip. I don't think he'd travel that far."

"Well, he may be in New Orleans for all I know. Of course, I devoutly hope he doesn't come. He's bad for our Sarah, too old and not of the right breeding."

"Now, Mother, don't be so fearful. I quite doubt he'll come here."

"Yes, but he knows she'll inherit part of the estate when I'm gone. He's after her money, not her heart. He'll just break it." Vivian wrung her hands and picked up the pen she had been using.

"But, Mother, he's already rich from his banking interests."

"There's greed in him. I see it. And he frequents...well, should I say it...dens of ill repute."

"To whom are you writing?"

"Judge Caldwell. I've asked him to be here at the party too, just in case that Feldcamp man shows up. He may be able to help us get rid of him."

"Is that really necessary, Mother? After all, we don't even know whether he'll be here."

"I think we should be prepared. There's no margin for error in this case."

"Perhaps, but don't fret. It may be much ado about nothing, as Shakespeare said." Deep down Robert was as concerned as his mother, and he knew she was right. Finally, he assured his mother, "If he shows up, don't worry. He'll not bother Sarah. I can assure you of that."

******

Teresa tossed and turned and her eyes popped open. She thought she'd been asleep, but then perhaps not. Had she been dreaming? She stared alternately at the ceiling and then at the narrow shaft of light on the floor. The bathroom door was slightly ajar, permitting the small lamp on the lavatory to cast a glowing sliver across the carpet to the chest on the opposite wall. Too much, Teresa thought, maybe there was too much light. No. She didn't like to sleep in total darkness. She needed boundaries because, without them, she felt claustrophobic. Suddenly, she was aware of something tickling her forehead. It was perspiration. Why was she sweating? The room was cool enough.

Then she sat upright in the bed as she heard a noise, far away but definite. Someone was crying. She looked over at Granger breathing evenly, quietly. Should she wake him? No, no. He probably wouldn't hear it anyway. The crying was getting a bit louder, as if the sobbing person were moving closer. She scurried into the bathroom, washed her face and returned. For a moment Teresa thought the crying had stopped, but then she heard it again. What should she do?

The bedroom door was closed, and only the very dim glow of a nightlight at the end of the hallway filtered through the gap at the bottom. After hurriedly donning a robe, Teresa carefully grasped the doorknob and turned slowly. She stuck her head out and looked both ways at an empty corridor. The sobbing was louder now. Marshaling her courage, she walked in measured steps toward the noise. The crying was coming from the old part of the house, from one of the bedrooms. Though she didn't want to admit it, Teresa knew it was Vivian, still inconsolably lamenting Sarah's death. As she wiped drops of sweat off her brow, she thought about the many tears Vivian had cried: millions upon millions. In the dim light she could see ahead of her the four steps that marked the juncture of the old house and the new wing. Once she crossed that threshold, she would be in Vivian's realm. The crying was quite loud and disturbing now, and she wondered what would happen if she actually reached its source.

Teresa stopped cold as she felt another presence. Out of the corner of her eye she detected a sudden, halting movement in an alcove off the hall. The niche was in dark shadow, but she could just discern the outline of someone standing there. Tall, almost hulking, the figure became motionless.

Then, without warning, "We've got to stop meeting like this."

Teresa jumped and muffled a yelp. It was Jack dressed in an ill-fitting robe that barely covered his knees.

She whispered loudly, "You almost gave me a heart attack." She took a deep breath and grasped his arm while she waited for the pounding in her chest to slow. "What are you doing up?" she asked.

"Well, I heard someone crying...."

"You hear it?" Teresa was shocked.

"The noise woke me up an hour ago. I finally had to see where it was coming from."

"It's coming from the east bedroom, Vivian's room."

"How do you know?"

"It's the crying Gloria told us about." Teresa had her wits back, and she was thinking more clearly now. "Remember?"

"I remember." Then, after a moment, "So, what do we do now?"

"I don't know. I'm afraid to go closer, but I think that's the only thing we can do."

"You know, this is way outside my comfort zone," said Jack in a loud whisper.

"You think it's inside mine?" Teresa barked back.

They stepped forward up the steps into the old part of the house and turned toward the east bedroom. The source of the crying was clearly inside the room, and they saw a faint light at the bottom of the closed door.

"What now?" whispered Jack.

As she swallowed and closed her eyes, Teresa instructed, "Open the door."

"You sure?"

"I think so." She squeezed her eyelids together even more tightly.

Jack moved his right hand slowly to the old knob and started to turn. Suddenly the sobbing ceased, and the light disappeared. They looked at each other.

"Go ahead. Open the door," said Teresa.

He turned the knob the rest of the way and pushed the heavy oak door forward. "What happened?" asked Jack as he peered at a dark, empty room.

"She's gone," replied Teresa.

"Where? Gone where?"

"I don't know. Gone to wherever spirits go, I guess. But she'll be back, and she'll keep coming until the mystery's solved. I just don't know why she's here now. It's July, not January." Teresa felt a rush of emotion coming over her. "Jack, I feel her sorrow. It's still here, very strong. I have to leave."

He took her hand and led her out the door and down the staircase to the kitchen.

"Here. Sit down for a while," he said.

They sat in silence at the kitchen table for a few moments.

"Jack, I have this feeling. I...I hate to say it...."

"Feeling?"

"I...I feel as if we've known each other before. In fact, I've had such a strong compulsion to...." She suddenly thought about Sister Catherine again. "Oh, I can't say it."

"What?" She felt Jack move closer to her and touch her shoulder. "I know what you mean, Teresa. I feel it too."

"We mustn't. We shouldn't."

"I know, but...but we could just leave here. Together. You know, we could just disappear, Teresa." He moved his hand down her arm slowly and started to pull her gently but firmly toward him.

"Jack, please. No."

He mumbled, "I...I can't help myself, Teresa." Then he pressed his lips to hers.

Suddenly the light in the kitchen came on. Teresa jumped back in her chair, and Jack sat upright.

"Well, what's going on down here?" It was Granger. Rubbing his eyes and yawning, he stammered, "I woke up and found the rest of the bed empty. Thought it might be near morning, but I guess not." He squinted his eyes at the digital clock on the counter. It was three thirty.

"Uh...I couldn't sleep," said Teresa as she smoothed her hair and tried to act nonchalant.

"Me neither," added Jack. "We heard some noises and ended up talking down here."

"Noises? What noises? And talking in the dark?"

"It was the crying, dear," said Teresa. "We heard the crying Gloria talked about. And it's not even January."

"You *both* heard it?"

"Yeah. Both of us," reported Jack.

Teresa quickly added, "When we agreed to stay the night, I figured I might hear it. But the time of the year isn't right, and then Jack heard it too. Strange, isn't it?"

"Just like everything over the last couple of days," said Granger as he sat down across the table. "So tell me what happened."

"Well, we both heard the crying coming from the east bedroom, and we got up and opened the door there," said Teresa.

"You mean you went inside the room?"

"Yes, but the crying suddenly stopped when we opened the door. There was some sort of light on in the room too, but it went out when we turned the doorknob."

"Boy, this thing gets weirder and weirder," said Granger. "I didn't hear a thing." He thought for a moment. "So I guess you two have something in common."

"Huh?" she asked absentmindedly. Teresa suddenly felt faint. Granger surely could not mistake the attraction to Jack. She wanted desperately to control her emotions, and Granger was the last person she would ever want to hurt.

"You know. You can both hear and see this stuff. How do you explain it, Jack? You're an engineer. How do you explain it?"

"I guess I can't. It's *inexplicable*, at least logically. But I'm totally convinced that something very unusual is going on. I can't deny it now that I've experienced it myself."

Teresa interjected, "You know what we need to do? We need to stay here in this house. Let's talk to Phyllis about it in the morning."

"I can't believe you're saying that." Granger frowned at Teresa. "Isn't this dangerous, especially for you?"

"Perhaps, but, as I've said before, I'll take the risk. It's the right thing to do."

While Teresa felt a strong resolve, she also knew there was now another, perhaps more perilous danger. She glanced at Jack and saw determination in his eyes as well. He smiled at her briefly and she averted her eyes. Somehow, this new danger was even more chilling than any generated by whatever restless spirits might still be wandering the halls of the old house.

Granger yawned again and stretched. "Well, it's still way too early for coffee. Let's go back to bed, dear. Think you can sleep now?"

"I don't really know, but I guess I have to try. Tomorrow, or should I say today, may be long."

"Good night again, Jack," said Granger as he reached toward Teresa.

"Night," replied Jack.

Teresa stood up and took Granger's hand. She saw Jack wink at her when she stole a quick glance. A couple of minutes later Jack followed them upstairs and tried to focus on the ceiling fan above his bed again. After a long time, he fell asleep.

Chapter Fourteen

The bright sunshine streaming through the windows in Jack's bedroom hit him squarely in the face. He opened first one eye, closed it, and then opened the other. For a few fleeting moments he didn't know where he was. Memories of his college days, when he prowled the beach at Malibu during Spring Break, came rushing back. There were many mornings then when he would awaken with the sun on his face and not know where he was. Those were good days filled with beautifully tanned, long-legged girls eager to spend their nights with a handsome Stanford man. Those were the best nights of his life. Through the fog in his brain, he stared again at that fan, still revolving slowly above him. No, he wasn't in Malibu, and he wasn't a college student. He suddenly remembered where he was and what had happened, and he groaned.

"Jam. Where's the raspberry jam, Gloria?" called Phyllis as she sat at the breakfast table with Teresa.

"I'll bring it, ma'am!"

"I just remembered," reported Phyllis, "that I have to go into town this morning with Gloria to pick out some decorations for the party this weekend. We have a caterer coming in with the food, but Gloria and Charles are going to do the decorating."

"Oh?" exclaimed Teresa. She still had the robe Phyllis gave her tied tightly around her waist. "Well, I think we'll be going to the county courthouse this morning." She hesitated to mention aloud the reason for their plans as Charles was in the kitchen.

"Oh, yes," said Phyllis in a hushed voice. "I'm quite interested in the outcome of your investigations there today."

Granger walked in and sat next to Teresa. "I found these pants and shirt in the closet, but they don't fit very well. Guess they belong to your son, Phyllis. I hope you don't mind."

"No, of course not."

"We'll go by the house to get some proper clothes this morning, and I'll call someone to fix the AC," said Granger.

Phyllis spooned a large portion of raspberry jam onto her toast. "Another thing. I've been thinking. Why don't you all just plan to stay here the rest of the week? It'll take a few days to get that air conditioner repaired anyway. You know how booked up the AC people get this time of year." She tilted her head and stared at nothing much in particular. "Funny thing: The only time air conditioners *can* go out is when you're using them. Besides, I'd love the company."

"Well...." Granger's protest was feeble.

"I won't take 'no' for an answer," said Phyllis.

"Well, okay. We appreciate the invitation. Thanks again, Phyllis," said Teresa. She flashed a quick smile at Granger.

"It's the least I can do for getting my house de-ghosted. Uh...I don't think that's a proper word, but you know what I mean."

"I hope we can do that. It'd solve our problems as well as yours," said Teresa. "We have a long way to go, but we made some progress last night."

"Last night?"

"Yes. Jack and I heard the crying in the east bedroom during the night. It was just like Gloria said."

"But it's not the right time of the year," protested Phyllis.

"I know. They...uh...the spirits, that is... must know we're here, and they're communicating off schedule, so to speak."

"Umm. I guess I'm not sure that's so good," said Phyllis as she munched on a slice of toast and dabbed her mouth with a napkin.

Gloria had overheard Teresa's words. "You heard the crying last night, ma'am?" she asked.

"Yes, Gloria. In the east bedroom, just as you told us."

"Ooh...that's scary. But at least I feel better that someone besides me heard it."

"Well, don't be afraid. The crying stopped when we were about to enter the room. So, actually, this...uh...ghost...is very shy."

"Still," said Gloria, "the whole thing frightens me."

"Good morning." Jack walked into the room in the uniform he had worn the night before.

"Why, colonel," said Phyllis in a wide grin, "I thought you'd resigned your commission."

Jack smiled back at her. "Oh, this is the only thing I could find quickly that I was willing to wear in public." He sat down at the table and watched Gloria pour him a cup of steaming coffee.

"What about that cute robe you had on last night in the kitchen?" snickered Granger.

"Well, that...uh...it wasn't exactly what I'd want to be seen wearing in broad daylight."

"I'm going over to the house this morning and get our clothes," said Granger. "And Phyllis has invited us to stay here the rest of the week, and we've accepted the invitation. Hope you agree."

Jack was picking strips of crisp bacon off a serving plate. "What? You think I'm stupid? Who wouldn't want to stay where it's cool and you get great breakfasts like this?" Suddenly he realized what he'd said. "Uh...I don't mean to cast any aspersions on your place, Granger."

"No need to apologize. I agree with you. This place certainly has a lot more going for it."

Phyllis swallowed a mouthful of coffee. "Well, I need to get ready to go into town. You all have the run of the house. I should be back in the afternoon, so let's plan to have tea in the parlor. Say about four? I haven't done that in years, and I think it'd be fun. Okay?"

"That'd be really nice," said Teresa. "Tea. It's so...uh...*civilized*." Then, after Phyllis left, "Well, what's our game plan for the day?"

Granger set down his cup. "First, I'll go get our clothes, that is if you trust me to get what you need. No reason for all of us to rifle around a hot house. I'll see if Phyllis can give me a ride on her way into town. Then I can drive my car back over here. That'd give us *two* cars we can use." He lowered his voice and moved his head closer to Teresa. "While I'm gone, maybe you can ask Charles a few questions...you know, before we go to the courthouse. Oh, don't forget about the key and the trunk. We can check that out too."

"Uh...are you sure you don't need some help with the clothes, dear," said Teresa as she glanced at Jack.

"Don't be silly. I've been around you long enough to know what to get for you, and I'll just bring all of Jack's stuff."

"Yeah, well," said Teresa as she bit down on a croissant. She just wasn't sure she wanted to be in the house with Jack while Granger was not around.

Granger was chewing the last bite of a banana when Phyllis came back into the room. "Phyllis, can I catch a ride with you to my place to pick up our clothes? I can drive back here in my own car."

"Oh, sure. See you guys later. By the way, Charles will be gone for a short while, too. He has to round up some groceries."

"Okay. We'll hold down the fort," said Jack. He sat quietly sipping coffee and nibbling on a piece of dry toast.

Soon only Jack and Teresa were left sitting in uncomfortable silence. After the tension had become almost unbearable, Teresa began to speak slowly. "Jack, I've been struggling with my conscience. I've thought about the promises I've made to Granger and the feelings I have for you. I've even struggled with one of my old teachers."

"Huh?"

"Sister Catherine. It's a long story."

Jack stared into her eyes. "You know I'm attracted to you, Teresa. Linda and I...well...our marriage is in trouble. But, you...you're so different from her. So much more desirable."

"Jack, there *is* a way to explain this immediate attraction we have for each other, but it conflicts with my Christian upbringing."

"How?"

"Well, I'm beginning to think we've known each other before."

"Before? When?"

"I don't know. Maybe back during Sarah's time."

"That's crazy, isn't it?"

"Of course, and it just doesn't make any sense, any logical sense anyway."

"Teresa, we live in the *twenty-first* century, not the nineteenth."

She suddenly sat upright. "Strange."

"Why so?" he asked with a puzzled look on his face.

"Granger said exactly the same thing to me a few days ago, almost word for word." She sat silently for a moment. Even though she had already accepted the reality of the paranormal events of the past few days, she had been jolted by Jack's comment. A strange chill crept up her back. "I...I think I'll go upstairs and clean up a bit. Maybe I can find something else to wear until Granger gets back."

******

Jack stared at himself in the mirror over the sink in his bathroom. He rearranged his disheveled hair, he examined his red eyes, and he rubbed the heavy stubble on his chin. Was he the same guy for whom those young girls at Malibu were so willing? Maybe Teresa was right about their knowing each other before. All he knew was that he needed to formulate a plan to win Teresa's favor. Somehow he had to have her. He took some deep breaths and washed his face. Opening the medicine cabinet, he found a razor, some new blades and shaving cream, a new toothbrush and some paste. Now he could freshen up and take a shower. He spent the next thirty minutes in the bathroom getting cleaned up, and he found some at least mildly more appropriate clothes in the closet. When he was finished dressing, he looked again in the mirror. Better, he thought, much better. Finally, he unlocked the bedroom door and walked slowly down the hall and the staircase toward the sound of voices. When he entered the kitchen, Charles was unloading groceries into the pantry, and Teresa was sitting at the breakfast table.

"Well, you're all cleaned up," she said. As she fumbled with the belt of the jeans she had found in her closet, she continued, "I found these things. I know they're a bit large, but it's the best I could do right now. Uh...Charles and I were just talking about Balfour and its history. Interesting stuff."

"Yeah, well, go on. I'm interested too," said Jack as he sat down at the small table. "Don't forget. I'm not from around here, so I don't know anything about Balfour."

"Well, I've lived around here all my life," said Charles. He scratched the crown of his head where the graying hair was particularly thin. "Guess I know just about everything about the place. I was born around the lake, near where my house is now, and I went to school at Consolidated over on the farm road. Class of '55. 'Course they've built a new building since I was there. I even went to junior college for a year or so, but I quit. Wasn't much of a student."

"What about your parents?" asked Teresa.

"Oh, they died by the time I was out of school."

"And other relatives?"

"Uh...they moved away over the years."

"So you've lived alone since your parents died?"

"Yes ma'am. Alone. 'Cept for a few animals here and there. They keep me company." Charles stopped what he was doing and frowned. "Say, why so many questions anyway?"

"Well," said Teresa, "you know Granger grew up around here too, but he never told me much history about the area. Funny. He's such a history nut about other times and places, but I don't think he ever knew you or your family."

"Probably not," replied Charles as he returned to his work. "I was quite a few years older, and I kept a real low profile."

"Mrs. Runyon said you've worked here for ten years," said Jack.

"That's right. Actually it's been more like eleven."

"You must've worked a lot of other places before you came here," stated Teresa.

"A lot of other places."

"Where? What kinds of jobs?"

"Well...mostly I've had jobs like the one here, but I've done other things too, like handyman, gardener, cook, even chauffeur."

"Chauffeur?"

Closing his eyes, Charles replied softly, "That chauffeur job was real nice. Got to drive some beautiful cars. Worked for an old lady over toward Longview." Then, with his eyes open, "She only needed me five days a week, so I could come home for my duties on the weekends."

"Duties? What kind of duties do you mean?" asked Jack.

"Oh, just family obligations. You know." He looked away.

"But you said you haven't had any family here in a long time."

"Well, uh...family's important even after they're gone."

"Hmm," said Teresa. "I suppose."

"After that I got this job."

"Why did you leave that one if you liked it so much?"

"The old lady died. Didn't need a chauffeur anymore."

Teresa smiled. "Yeah, well, I guess not. How do you like it here with the Runyons?"

"Like it fine. The Runyons are real good people. They treat me, well, like family, and I love this house."

Teresa looked around the room. "It's a gorgeous place all right. Uh...Charles, I guess you've explored every nook and cranny of this house over the past ten...er eleven...years."

"I suppose."

"Any interesting tidbits about the house that we wouldn't have learned from taking just the usual twenty-five cent tour?"

"Tidbits?"

"You know: Strange occurrences, secret rooms, skeletons in the closet."

"Can't think of any. Of course, it's an old house. Dates from the middle 1800's, you know."

"So, a house as old as this one must have some juicy history."

"Wouldn't know about that. Not much of a history person. But I *do* like this house. Kind of talks to you." Charles had completed his chore and was staring, trancelike, toward the window.

"Talks? What do you mean?" asked Jack.

He suddenly disengaged from the trance. "Well, enough about all that. Guess you didn't learn much about Balfour, just about me. Pretty boring. Uh...now, if you'd excuse me, I have some other work to do."

"Of course," said Teresa. "Enjoyed talking to you." With that, Charles left through the back door and walked toward the garage.

Chapter Fifteen

"Where *are* you guys?" Granger called out from the foyer. Teresa yelled back at him. "In here, in the kitchen."

"Give me some help with the luggage."

Teresa and Jack dutifully helped Granger carry the bags upstairs to the bedrooms, and they all changed clothes.

"Charles is hiding something," said Teresa after they all reconvened in the parlor.

"I couldn't tell that from what he said," responded Jack. "How do you know?"

"Well, it's not in *what* he said but *how* he said it—the inflection of his voice, his body language."

"Your reasoning is pretty squashy, dear," said Granger.

Teresa shrugged. "So what else is new? This whole thing is squashy. There's something he doesn't want us to know, and it's something about the house and his relationship to it."

Granger's frustration with his wife's hunches and mysterious feelings boiled over. "Fine. I accept that you're clairvoyant, but how are we going to find out what he's hiding? We have to have some concrete evidence here, not just feelings."

Teresa backed down a bit. "Well, I suppose our visit to the courthouse might give us some evidence."

"So, why are we wasting time?" asked Jack. "Let's go."

They all piled into Granger's Jaguar, which he affectionately called his "mid-life crisis car". Her mind in a fog, Teresa hardly said a word as they drove the ten miles into town.

The new courthouse was located only about a block from the old one Granger and Teresa had visited a few days before. Sleek and modern, the new building was much different from the nineteenth century structure. Instead of honey-colored oak, the foyer was paved with hard, gray granite, the doors were framed with cold metal instead of warm natural wood, and even the carpet was synthetic. But the offices hummed with spinning hard drives and clicked with ergonomic keyboards. Interconnected by an almost totally electronic control system, the offices in the new building were tangible testaments to modern technology.

"Quite a place. When was this thing built?" asked Jack as they walked into the large first-floor entry hall.

"Only about three years ago. I remember there was a big brouhaha about how much it was going to cost. Went way over budget. Of course, like most things, it's a scandal at the time, but within a few years, everyone forgets the controversy. I think building it was good, despite the cost. Of course, I don't pay much tax here anymore, so I guess I can't say much."

They took the elevator up to the third floor records office where they were directed to a set of computers lining the wall.

"Let's do a search on Charles to see when and where he was born," said Granger.

"That sounds good," replied Jack.

"Let's see. Breck...Charles Breck. Hmm. Here it is. Born 1939 in a local hospital." He frowned. "That's funny. Didn't you say Charles told you he was in the Class of '55?"

"That's right," said Teresa.

"But that couldn't be unless he moved ahead a grade or two," replied Granger as he scratched his head.

Teresa was doing the math. "Thirty-nine plus eighteen...that's fifty-seven. Class of '57...or maybe Class of '56 if he started early. How could he have been born in 1939 and graduate from high school in 1955?"

"It doesn't make sense. He said he wasn't much of a student, so I don't think he skipped any grades," said Jack.

Granger thought for a moment. "Let me check something else." He logged onto the death records database. "Let's see if Charles Breck is still with us."

"Why are you doing that?" asked Teresa.

"He wants to see if Charles is using a dead person's name," said Jack.

Jack and Teresa huddled behind Granger.

"Well, here it is," said Granger. "Charles Breck. Died 1959 at the county hospital. No next of kin listed. Write down this social security number. We can check with Phyllis to see what number Charles is using."

"So, what's going on?" asked Teresa as she scribbled down the nine digits.

"Charles may be using this Breck guy's name and social security number as a cover-up," said Jack. "He may have stolen this guy's identity."

"What's he trying to cover up?"

"Why, his real name, of course. Breck's not his real name."

"But why would he want to do that?"

"For some reason, he doesn't want anyone to know who he really is," said Granger.

Teresa was still puzzled. "But people who do that are usually hiding from the law, aren't they?"

"That's one reason. Other reasons might be to avoid creditors or to get out of paying alimony or child support. But maybe it's something else."

"For instance?" she asked.

"Well, in this case it might have something to do with the house," said Granger.

Now she was even more confused. "Okay. You lost me again."

"You're the clairvoyant person around here. You ought to know the reason."

Teresa was getting frustrated. "Well, I don't."

"Maybe his name would give away his connection with the house."

"Oh...you mean like maybe he's a Feldcamp or a Bollinger?" asked Teresa.

"Now you're getting it," said Granger.

"Umm. That might explain it. But, if it does, he sure went to great lengths to conceal his identity," said Jack.

"That's true," agreed Teresa. "But it would've been easy for him if his parents were dead, all of his relatives had moved away, and he had no friends. So, no one would be the wiser. And the real Charles Breck didn't have any family either. Except, what about the people who knew him when he was growing up—like his classmates?"

Granger thought for a minute. "Well, he was always a loner. Maybe he changed his name while he lived elsewhere. Then, later, when he moved back here, he kept a low profile and no one was the wiser."

"Far-fetched, but maybe," said Jack. "So, let's put this theory to the computer test."

"You mean search for the names Feldcamp and Bollinger?" asked Granger.

"Exactly."

"This is good stuff," exclaimed Teresa. "I'm starting to believe this really *is* a Sherlock Holmes situation."

Granger searched the birth records for the name Feldcamp, and Jack searched for Bollinger.

"No real match on Feldcamp," said Granger. "No Feldcamp born during that time period, except Jed. He's listed, but he was born in '34. So he would've been out of school a few years before Charles."

"Aha," said Jack excitedly. "Look. A Bollinger was born in 1937—exactly the right year. His name is Craig."

"Could that be Charles?"

"Maybe."

"Let's check death records for his parents." After a few keystrokes, Granger exclaimed, "Yep. One died in '57 and the other in '58, about the time Charles...er Craig...graduated from high school."

"Well, do you think this is conclusive?" asked Teresa.

"*I* think so," said Jack.

"What about you, Granger. Is this concrete enough for *you*?"

"Okay, dear, okay. I bow to your prowess once again. It's good enough for me. Let's print a copy of this information to show Phyllis. She'll be quite interested."

"That she will," said Jack.

During the drive back to the house they discussed alternatives for handling the situation.

"Well," said Teresa, "I don't think we should approach Charles at this point."

"So, what do we do, dear?" Granger asked.

"To stretch a cliché, I think we should play it by ear and, I might add, by eye. I mean, we should tell Phyllis and then all keep our eyes and ears open to see what Charles does."

"How do we know Phyllis isn't already aware of his...how can I say it...clandestine identity?" asked Jack.

Teresa looked at him with wide eyes. "Oh, come on. If she knew, why wouldn't she have told us? It doesn't make sense."

"I don't really know," replied Jack, "but none of this stuff makes sense."

Teresa shook her head. "I can't think about that right now. In any case, we should be as discreet as possible with this information," said Teresa.

"I agree," responded Granger.

By the time they reached the house once again, Phyllis had returned.

"Have any luck?" asked Phyllis.

"More than we even hoped for," replied Teresa. "We sort of hit the jackpot."

"Jackpot? What do you mean?"

Teresa detailed the discoveries at the courthouse as they all sat in the parlor. Phyllis rolled her eyes when they showed her the deceased Charles Breck's social security number.

"Is that the number Charles is using?" asked Teresa.

"Uh...yes. I think so."

Teresa was trying to detect a reaction in Phyllis's manner when they told her about Charles. She had hoped for some kind of sign, some type of emotion that would communicate whether she was already aware of his real identity.

"Boy, for some reason, I think the tsetse flies are buzzing around here," said Granger through a long, slow yawn. "I can hardly keep my eyes open."

"Me too," agreed Teresa. "Maybe we should rest for a while and regroup here in time for tea."

"Good idea," said Phyllis. "I'm worn out from shopping in the heat this morning. Besides, I need time to think about this information you guys came up with. I'm having a hard time swallowing it all in one gulp."

"Where's Charles now?" asked Granger.

"Picking some vegetables from the garden out back," replied Phyllis.

Teresa perked up. "You have a vegetable garden?"

"Oh yes. That broccoli you ate last night was from our summer crop, and we have a rather large flower garden too."

"I haven't been out back. Granger, later, when it's cooler, let's take a walk out there. I'd like to see it."

"Okay. In fact, you and I have some things to talk about." Then, as he stifled another yawn, he added, "But, for now, the tsetse flies are swarming."

Chapter Sixteen

"The accounts, Mother. I can help you with them." Robert was looking at piles of papers stacked all over the desk in front of Vivian.

"I don't need any help, dear. When I'm gone you can take over the accounts. Until then, I'm in charge."

"But Mr. Grover told me that we're behind in our payments to him, and I know you sold two field slaves the other day. It's not like you. A few years ago you wanted to free them all."

"I know, I know. It's just...uh... a bit of a cash flow problem. Now don't be bothered about such things."

"Mother, I'm over twenty years old now—old enough to know about what's going on. Father was showing me things even when I was only fifteen."

"Entirely too young. You were entirely too young then. I told your father what I thought. He was a headstrong man, you know." She thought for a few moments. "But I loved him dearly." She sighed.

"But, Mother..."

"I'll handle the accounts, dear," interrupted Vivian. "Why, even the cotton brokers in Jefferson say I'm doing a good job."

"Yes, they did, but that was last year. What about this year? Things are different now."

"No, no. I'll have none of that talk. We're doing just fine. Just fine."

******

Teresa awoke from a fitful sleep. The dream that had just flashed by was as disturbing as the visions. Was it yet another communication from the past or merely a figment of her own fertile imagination? She looked at Granger, still napping, lying next to her, and her thoughts turned to the handsome stranger from San Francisco.

While she loved Granger, she was almost overwhelming attracted to Jack. The two emotions were so contradictory that she wondered how they could coexist. After all, her whole life had been built around the marital relationship with her husband. She wanted their union to be strong and enduring, close and supportive, and, perhaps most of all, loving and trusting. Ah, that was the problem: trust. She herself was compromising the mutual honesty that had been built up over the many years of their marriage. The desire for Jack was anathema to all her ideals and to everything her mother had taught her. Somehow, she had to keep her feelings for him secret.

"Granger," she whispered loudly, "it's almost four. Time for tea."

"Ugh," he groaned. "Seems like it's only been a few minutes. You sure of the time?" He squinted at the clock on the nightstand and grunted again.

They found Jack already downstairs.

"I thought I was really sleepy, but I hardly closed my eyes," Jack said. "Too many thoughts ricocheting around in my brain." He glanced at Teresa. "You know how conflicted the situation is right now."

"Uh...yes, of course," said Teresa, "the whole thing is very confusing."

Phyllis almost bounced into the room. "Well, here we all are. Ready for tea?"

"You must've had a good nap," said Granger as he stifled a yawn.

"Actually I did. I don't normally sleep in the afternoon, but I'm glad I did today. It's surprising how much difference just a couple of hours of sleep can make."

"Yeah, well, it may have made a difference for some, but not for others," grumbled Granger.

"Before Charles comes in," reported Teresa, "I think you all should know about a dream I had while I was napping...at least I think it was a dream."

"Dream?" asked Jack.

"Yes. I dreamed that the Bollingers were having some financial difficulties and that, because of the problems, Robert wanted to take the handling of the financial accounts away from Vivian."

"So?" asked Granger.

"Well, she wouldn't let him. She wanted to handle everything herself, and he was definitely not happy about it."

Phyllis was sitting on the edge of the couch. "What else?"

"That's it."

"That's all?" continued Phyllis.

"Yep. At that point I woke up."

"Not much information, but, assuming this is another valid communication, it does tell us one thing," said Granger.

"What?" asked Teresa.

"Well, if the family was having financial problems, Vivian might have been more receptive to Sarah's marriage to Lance. He was a rich banker, and access to his money would certainly have helped bail them out."

"Yes, dear, but Vivian didn't like Lance. Remember the ladies of the evening and the gambling?"

"I remember. But she might have changed her mind because of those family financial problems, and maybe Robert had a different opinion anyway. Based on what you said happened in your dream, he didn't always agree with his mother."

"Hmm. No, he didn't."

"Well, we may not have the puzzle put together, but at least we're collecting a lot of pieces," said Phyllis.

Charles and Gloria brought three pots of different types of tea, a plate of finger sandwiches and another of scones with butter and raspberry jam.

"The scones are from an old family recipe. My maiden name was MacDonald, so I come by my love of these things naturally, I guess. In fact, my mother told me one time that my great-great grandmother…or was it great-great-great? Anyway, she personally brought the scone recipe over here with her from Scotland. That story is probably apocryphal, but I like to tell it anyway. Makes the scones taste better."

"Umm. You must be right," reported Granger as he swallowed, "because they *are* wonderful."

Jack smeared a glob of butter and a layer of jam on a scone and took a bite. "Yep. I agree."

Phyllis glanced toward the entry and lowered her voice. "Well, now that Charles and Gloria are back in the kitchen, we can probably discuss things again."

"Actually," said Teresa, "I'd rather just enjoy the tea and snacks for a while."

Phyllis shook her head in agreement. "I would too, but, like I said, we have a lot of puzzle pieces to put together, and I have a feeling we don't have them all yet."

Teresa couldn't help wondering whether Phyllis herself was one of those undiscovered pieces. "Well, the main things we need to consider right now are Charles and the trunk key."

"Right. So, how do we proceed?" asked Granger.

Teresa immediately responded. "I think Charles will tip his hand somehow, especially when he realizes we might have the trunk key. We only have to wait."

"Patience: that's the one thing I'm running out of," said Granger as he wiped a sticky bit of jam off his fingers.

"Me too," agreed Jack. "I have a reservation on a flight early Sunday to get back to San Francisco in time for a reception there that evening."

Holding up her right hand, Teresa assured Jack, "I know, I know. But we still have a couple of days, and the party's Saturday night. Just give Charles a little more rope."

"Okay. But how about the key?" asked Phyllis.

"Yes, the key," repeated Teresa. "Good question."

"Well, let's take some time this evening to give the basement a good going over," said Granger. "We should be able to check out at least all the *accessible* trunks."

"Good," said Teresa. "By the way, where *is* that key?"

"I hid it," said Phyllis. "I didn't want to chance losing it."

"Later," said Granger. "Later we'll check out the trunks. For now, I'll have another cup of that Earl Grey."

Phyllis topped off the cups all around, and they relaxed for a time in idle conversation while eating the rest of the scones and sandwiches. Afterwards, they sampled the cookies and sweet tarts Gloria served for dessert.

******

As afternoon melted into evening, Teresa and Granger ventured into the garden behind the house. A rain-cooled breeze was blowing off a nearby shower, and dark clouds hid the sun intermittently. She could see that he was wearing his "frowny face", the name she gave to his expression when he had something serious on his mind. She knew he was thinking about Jack, a subject she really didn't want to discuss. Maybe if she diverted his attention.... "Look at all the vegetables. No wonder the broccoli was so good last night." She pointed toward a large rectangular patch furrowed row upon row. "Boy, they have carrots, tomatoes, peppers, corn...and is that squash?" She thought she was succeeding. "And over there," she continued, "is the flower garden." She pointed toward a stone path that pierced a narrow gap in a low hedge. "Let's go see. I've always wanted to have a flower garden behind our house."

The flower garden contained multicolored roses, azaleas, chrysanthemums, petunias, oleanders, honeysuckle, begonias and verbenas at various stages of blooming.

She quickly continued as she took Granger's hand. "The air smells so good—the flowers, the grass, the cool breeze off the storm. I just love it."

After they had walked a while in silence, Granger stopped, took her by the arm and turned to face her. "Teresa," said Granger, "I...I hate to bring this up, but I have to."

"What." Teresa could see that he was dead serious because there was no hint of a smile on his face. At the same time, however, he wasn't looking at her directly in the eye as he usually did when he was sure of himself.

He glanced down, then up at the sky. "I know what's happening between you and Jack."

"Happening?"

"Yes. Don't lie about it." His face was now fixed and his words crisp and distinct. "I know you're attracted to him, and I saw what was going on in the kitchen last night."

"Granger, I...." Teresa grasped one of her hands with the other.

"Wait. Let me finish," he interrupted. "Teresa, I've always trusted you, but I'm starting to wonder." His voice was even stronger now. "I used to have no doubts at all about our relationship, and now I'm literally filled with uncertainty. I know you've always resented me for not wanting another child, and that resentment's driven a wedge between us. These visions, this mystery, have only made things worse. I can only hope this attraction between you and Jack will disappear when the mystery is solved."

"Can I talk now?"

Softer, "Of course." His hands were shaking.

Teresa took a deep breath and felt an unexpected rush of courage. "Well, I have to admit it. You're right. There *is* an attraction. Nothing's really happened between Jack and me, but I confess that there's something. I can't explain it and, yes, it *is* related to the mystery. I...I know this sounds weird, but it's possible Jack and I knew each other before."

"Before? What do you mean?"

"Like in a previous life. And, don't laugh. I know it doesn't make any sense, and, based on my religious training, I have to reject the whole idea. I hope it's *not* true, but I just can't shake the feeling."

"Well, uh...I guess I didn't expect that. I'm not sure...." His voice trailed off. Teresa saw the shock and disbelief in Granger's eyes.

"I wish I could use my clairvoyance to see what's going to happen, but I can't. All I can say is that, deep down, I'm still devoted to you and only to you. I'm just struggling right now. I don't want to lose you. You can be assured of that."

"Well, I have to admit I *do* think your explanation is...uh...well, unusual. At the same time, I...I guess it makes me feel better." He quickly added, "But not *much* better."

Teresa felt limp. "I can understand that. It's just that I'm not in control of this thing. I wish I were, but I'm not. Only time will tell me...that is...*us* how it's going to work out. I think what we need to concentrate on right now is solving this mystery as soon as possible. After that, we'll have to handle the fallout, whatever it might be." She took his hand again, squeezed it, kissed him tenderly and said in almost a whisper, "Okay, dear?"

Granger felt boxed in. He couldn't just abandon Teresa. He, like her, had invested the major portion of his life in their marriage, and he didn't want to see it crumble. At the same time, he was bristling inside at the thought of his wife with Jack. Defense mechanisms rooted in ages-old primal instincts were boiling up inside him. He thought how several thousand years ago he would have just thrown Jack off some cliff and dragged Teresa back to his cave, and that would be that. But he had to resist such unsophisticated urges. He was, after all, a well-developed, extremely civilized modern man in a caring relationship, not some barbaric pre-Neanderthal defending his territory.

Thankfully, Teresa granted him the gift of silence for several minutes while they walked very slowly along the stone path. Finally, he spoke. "You know, these flowers really *are* pretty."

"Huh?"

"Remember the lightning bugs?"

"Uh...yes, of course."

"Remember how I said they were inconsequential...that my musings about them really didn't matter?"

"Yes."

"Well, maybe I was wrong."

"What do you mean?"

"I mean maybe even the little things are important."

"Huh?"

"Think how insignificant the mystery of what happened to Sarah is in the grand scheme of things, yet she's still influencing our lives even though she's been gone for a hundred and fifty years. Her life and death were, in the cosmic sense, extremely unimportant events on a small planet in a tiny solar system in a remote corner of one of millions of galaxies. I could go on and on. But she has significance to us today and, I'm confident, to God. Even the lightning bugs are important to God."

"Yes. I believe that's true."

He could tell by the puzzled look on her face that she still didn't understand what he meant.

"So, if it's important to God, shouldn't it be important to *me*...to *us*? And, if that's true, we all need to see this thing through to the end."

"Does that mean you'll give me the benefit of the doubt...for now?" she asked as they stopped and sat down on a concrete bench in the midst of the flowers.

"Yes, dear, it does. I want our marriage to continue as it was before all this began. I'll do everything I can to help you solve the mystery as quickly as possible. You know, time's important when you deal with the heart."

As Teresa tilted her head to rest on Granger's shoulder, a tear trickled down her cheek and onto his hand. "I know, I know."

Chapter Seventeen

The sun had disappeared below the horizon by the time they all gathered at the base of the stairs in the stuffy, cluttered basement. Armed with flashlights and a couple of lanterns, they scanned the area nearby to find a trunk that could be reached without having to move stacks of boxes and artifacts.

"Over here," said Teresa. She pointed at a large object under a pile of two-by-fours.

"That's one of 'em," Phyllis confirmed. "If you guys will stack the lumber to the side, I'll try the key."

Granger and Jack unloaded the long pieces of wood off the trunk and backed away to allow Phyllis access to the lock. "Nope. Doesn't fit this one."

"Now what?" asked Jack.

"Here's another one," yelled Teresa.

After Phyllis saw where Teresa was pointing, she said, "That's not the one. The thing's not locked anyway because I looked through it several years ago. All that's in there are old maps."

"Oh, I want to see," said Granger. "They might be of some value."

Phyllis opened the lid and coughed. "Ugh. This dust is bad. I hope I don't aggravate my allergies."

Granger rifled through the stack of papers inside. "You're right. Some of these things are *really* old...hand-drawn. Look at this one." He held up a yellowed piece of paper in the beam of his flashlight. "It looks like a map of the Balfour area. Hmm. Hard to say when the map was drawn." He studied it for another several seconds.

"Granger, put that back. It's not what we're looking for," ordered Teresa.

"There's an arrow pointing out a blacksmith's shop near the creek. There's an old dirt road out that way now. And here's a place labeled 'mercantile'. Must be a general store. Oh, and here's a bank. This thing must date from the 1800's, but no telling exactly."

"Okay, okay, let's move on," reiterated Teresa impatiently.

Granger carefully replaced the map and closed the lid. "I want to inventory all these maps. Could be some good stuff here. You mind if I do that, Phyllis?"

"No. Not at all. I'm not into maps and such, and I probably wouldn't recognize anything of value anyway. I guess I always thought of this stuff as old junk, but maybe I was wrong."

"Yikes," exclaimed Jack as he aimed his lantern toward a dark corner.

"What is it?" asked Phyllis.

"Looks like an old rat nest. No current occupants, thank goodness."

Phyllis shrugged her shoulders. "No telling what's down here. Probably ought to herd some hungry cats through this place. They might find it really interesting...and appetizing." She chuckled.

******

Robert dragged the heavy leather bag across the floor toward the old oak trunk in the corner. He took the key out of his pocket, turned it in the lock and lifted the ponderous lid. After he set down the lantern he'd been carrying, he worked to make room inside and heaved the jingling sack into the opening. It landed on the bottom with a thud and the tinkling of metal against metal. Just at that moment, he picked up another shiny object, looked at it briefly and placed it gently in the trunk.

"Robert," Vivian called from the door at the top of the stairs. "Are you down there?"

He knew he had to avoid getting caught in the basement again because it would arouse his mother's suspicions. He blew out the lantern's flame and sat quietly in the dark.

"Robert! Robert, I think you're there." After he heard some unintelligible muffled words, another figure came down the steps with a lantern. It was Peter, the butler.

"Missah Robert, you down here?" Peter called. "Yo' momma wants yo' to come upstairs." Peter walked slowly around the room. "Please come out, Missah Robert."

"Peter," Vivian called from the top of the stairs, "is he down there?"

"I don't see 'im, Missus. Nobody here. Can I come out now?"

Robert could barely make out Peter's wrinkled, leathery face as he weaved his way through the clutter.

"All right, Peter, you can come on back upstairs," yelled Vivian. "I guess he's not down there. Where *is* that boy?" Her voice trailed off as she walked away.

Peter headed back toward the stairs. As he turned he looked in the direction of the motionless Robert. He smiled, raised his lantern and winked. Robert smiled back and breathed a sigh of relief. Peter had not given him away, so now he could finish his work.

******

"It's in the far corner," said Teresa as she pointed toward a dark part of the huge room. "The trunk we're looking for is over there."

"There?" queried Granger as he pointed. "That area is really covered with junk. How do you know that's where it is? There are a couple of others we could get to more easily. Why don't we look at them first?"

"No. That's the one. I know," explained Teresa blankly.

"Huh?"

"Robert put something into that trunk over there: a large leather bag full of something."

"Full of what?" asked Jack.

"I'm not sure. But whatever it was clanged and jingled, like coins."

"Coins? You mean money?" asked Phyllis.

"Maybe."

"Well, even if that's true," said Granger, "the coins might be gone now."

Teresa countered, "That's right, but we have to check."

"Okay," Jack said as he glanced at Teresa, "let's get busy. I guess you say 'frog', then we jump."

To get to the location Teresa had identified, Granger and Jack had to move a crate of old toys, several large pieces of lumber, stacks of old books and over a dozen heavy boxes and barrels.

"Whew," said Granger as he wiped his dripping forehead with a handkerchief. "I hope whatever is in that trunk is worth all this effort."

"Yeah," agreed Jack. He looked directly at Teresa and Phyllis and grinned. "If it isn't, then next time you two do all the heavy lifting."

Soon they had cleared a narrow path surrounded by the heaps they had created. At the end, near the corner of the basement, they found a large oak trunk.

"Well, there *is* a trunk, it's old, and it's covered with dust," Granger reported.

Jack pulled on the latch. "And it's locked. Question is whether the key we have will open it."

"And I have the key," said Phyllis. "Let me at it."

They all stepped back to allow Phyllis to come forward. Granger trained the beam from his flashlight on the lock, and Phyllis inserted the key.

"Ugh. Doesn't work." She strained to turn it.

"Be gentle," recommended Granger. "Sometimes a little tenderness goes a long way." Their laughter broke the tension.

She took a deep breath and turned it more slowly. The metal clicked into place and made a 360-degree arc inside the keyhole.

"Well, that's it," said Phyllis. Her pulse was racing, and she could swear she heard Teresa's heart beating fast too. "I guess we can open it now."

Jack stepped up. "Help me, Granger. This lid looks like it weighs a ton."

Granger helped Jack push the squeaking iron-banded camelback lid up against the basement wall, and they trained the beams from all four lights into the dark jaws of the opening.

"Looks like flowers," said Phyllis. "Old, dried up flowers are piled on top." She reached in and pulled out several long stems. "Roses, I think...at least they used to be." Phyllis counted them. "Twelve. An even dozen."

Teresa was touched. "Boy, I feel almost as if we've desecrated a tomb. I wonder who put the roses in here and why."

"They must've meant a lot to someone to save them this way," offered Phyllis.

"No feelings about them, dear?" asked Granger.

Teresa was still carefully placing each of the twelve flowers on the floor such that they would not be disturbed. "Not really. I kind of feel numb."

Jack looked back into the trunk. "Okay, what next?"

Granger pulled out a faded, crumbling newspaper. "Let's see. New Orleans *Picayune* from January 1855. Why, that's the month Sarah died."

"Wow. This is giving me goose bumps," said Phyllis.

"Maybe we shouldn't be looking at all of this," warned Granger. "I'm starting to feel like Teresa."

Teresa quickly spoke up. "Maybe. But we have to go on. This is the only way to solve the mystery once and for all."

"Okay, dear. You're running the show, but be careful," said Granger.

"Here are some decks of cards," reported Jack. "And several pairs of dice. Oh, look at this old corked bottle." He examined the label. "Booze. Nineteenth century booze." He tilted the bottle to show that it was still half full of amber liquid.

"Funny how all this stuff is so neatly packed," Phyllis observed. "It's as if someone placed each item in here very deliberately—just so."

Granger focused his flashlight on a small black book. "Hmm. A Bible." He picked it up and opened it. "Look at the inscription," he said as he pointed to faded handwriting inside the front cover.

"Sarah Bollinger, from Mother, Christmas 1854," read Teresa. "Guess she didn't have much time to use it." She tenderly placed it on the floor next to the flowers.

"It's a daguerreotype," said Jack. He picked up a small flat plate of what appeared to be glass with a ghostly image on it. "Wonder who it is."

Phyllis squinted at the faded portrait of a young girl. "Based on the other things we've found here, it's probably Sarah herself."

"This is too much," said Teresa. Tears were starting to well from her eyes. "We may be actually looking at a picture of Sarah. It's chilling." She wanted desperately to stop. She wanted to put everything carefully back exactly as they had found it, to close and lock the lid, and to leave Balfour forever. To go on was almost physically painful. She groaned, "I...I don't know."

"You okay, dear?" asked Granger as he put his hand on her shoulder.

Jack reiterated, "Are you sure you're all right, Teresa?"

"I think so. I'm hanging in there, but barely." She rubbed a handkerchief across her face and blew her nose.

"I understand what you mean," said Phyllis. "To think all this has been here for all these years undisturbed. We never knew where…I mean, we never knew about all this stuff. Now I'm starting to comprehend the history of this place."

Granger turned his attention back to the contents of the trunk. "Hmm. A mirror, a comb and…ha! Look at this: a chamber pot. Well, I guess we know what this was for." He smiled and, for the first time since they opened the trunk, Teresa smiled too.

Jack flashed his light toward one corner. "There are a couple of other books in here. Hmm…Dickens: <u>A Christmas Carol</u> and <u>Oliver Twist</u>. Guess they were best-sellers back then." He hesitated a moment. "This one doesn't have a title. Oh…." He hesitated. "It's a diary."

"A diary?" asked Phyllis.

Jack glanced at a couple of the entries. "It's Sarah's diary." He quickly turned to the first page. "First entry is in 1850, when she was thirteen."

Teresa could hardly say it: "And the date of the last entry?"

Jack thumbed toward the back of the journal and adjusted the lantern he had set on the floor. "January 8th 1855."

"The day before she died," reported Teresa.

"What a find!" exclaimed Granger.

"Kind of the ultimate history book," said Phyllis. "I guess it'll tell us the whole story, at least from Sarah's point of view."

"I guess," said Teresa. She took the diary from Jack and quietly put it in her pocket. "Let's go on."

"Well, there are lots and lots of clothes: dresses, petticoats, some nineteenth century unmentionables. At least I think that's what they are," said Granger. Suddenly he stopped short. "The dress on the bottom of the stack. It's blue."

Phyllis squinted at it in the imperfect light. "It's blue satin."

"You mean *the* blue satin dress?" asked Jack.

"Hmm. Wait. There's something else about the dress."

"What?" asked Teresa.

Granger looked at her. "It's all torn; it's in shreds. All the other dresses look perfect, but this one is messed up." A chill went up

Granger's spine. "And...uh...it has stains on it, lots of them. I'm no forensic expert, but the stains look like dried blood to me."

"Blood?" asked Teresa. She was shaking. "*Her* blood?"

Granger took Teresa's ice-cold right hand. "Teresa. Calm down." He saw that she was trembling. "Listen, guys, uh...we need to stop. Teresa can't stay down here any longer."

"But we haven't found the sack yet," said Jack. Then, after a moment, "On second thought, let's just go back upstairs and worry about that later."

"Yes, let's," agreed Phyllis quickly.

Granger led Teresa up the stairs while Jack and Phyllis closed the trunk and left the things that had been taken out on the floor nearby. Soon they were all sitting in the parlor staring blankly at one another. At first, no one spoke. Nothing could have prepared them for the items they had found. They were all emotionally drained and physically exhausted.

Finally, Phyllis broke the silence. "Well, I guess we have some concrete proof now."

"Yeah. Concrete enough for me," said Jack. "And I need a drink to settle my nerves."

"Yes," agreed Phyllis. Though Charles had left early, Gloria was still in the kitchen, and Phyllis called her to bring glasses and a large pitcher of margaritas. "Let's get our minds off all of this tonight."

"Are you all right, Teresa?" asked Granger.

Almost trance-like, Teresa replied, "I think I'll be okay. Just give me some time." After a moment she added, "And a few drinks."

Gloria brought in the cold beverages, and Phyllis poured the green liquid into large glasses. They each inhaled their first drink and sipped on the second. Finally, after several minutes, they began to relax. The day had been long, the night was only just beginning, and they all knew the mystery had only been proved, not solved.

Chapter Eighteen

Almost in a whisper, Phyllis excitedly held the phone to closely and reported, "George, we found a trunk in the basement with old stuff from Sarah's time."
"What?" asked George. "We must have a bad connection."
"I said we found it...in the basement."
"It's full of all kinds of things, but not what we're looking for."
"Do they suspect anything?"
"I...I don't think so. 'Course, they *do* know about Charles. What do you think I should do?"
"Play along, just play along. That strategy's been working so far, despite having to reveal Charles's identity. I'll be home Friday, but don't let on you know anything. Okay?"
"Okay. See you then, honey."
"Bye."

******

After sleeping soundly through the night, Teresa sensed a high-pitched, annoying noise that stopped, then started, then stopped again. Through the filter of semi-consciousness, she realized that it was the sound of a telephone ringing. Then she didn't hear it anymore, but she perceived a far-off voice. Though she couldn't quite make out the chatter, she heard the word 'George'. She turned over toward Granger, but he was already gone. Now wide awake, she sat up in bed and rubbed her eyes. She had a splitting headache. Then she recalled what had happened the night before: the discoveries in the basement, the margaritas in the parlor and, only vaguely, the plodding climb up the stairs to the bedroom. All of a sudden, she realized she was ravenous. She had not eaten since teatime fifteen hours earlier.

"There's the sleepyhead," said Phyllis as Teresa sat down at the dining room table. "You must be starving. Granger just beat you downstairs."

"I'm pretty hungry. How long have you guys been up?"

"Oh, only half an hour or so," said Phyllis.

"How's your head?" asked Granger.

"My head?"

"You have a headache, don't you?"

"Why, yes. How'd you know?"

"You always do after drinking a bit too much. I warned you last night but you wouldn't listen."

"Huh?"

"Guess you don't remember. I barely do either."

"No, I don't, but I believe you. I do have quite a head-throbber. I just hope eating helps."

"If not, there's some aspirin in the kitchen cabinet," said Phyllis.

They all were silent for a few minutes as they downed their breakfast. Then, Phyllis spoke up. "George called from London this morning. He'll be home tomorrow evening."

"Tomorrow?" queried Teresa.

"Yes. Friday evening. I updated him on what we found yesterday. Of course, I didn't have time to tell him everything, but I think he got the gist of the story. He said now he has a ghost story to rival the ones told by all those 'stiff upper lip' British guys he's working with over there."

"What about your children?" asked Jack.

"Oh, they should be storming in late tomorrow too. One's coming from Dallas, the other from New Orleans. In fact, I think Julia, that's my daughter in New Orleans, is flying to Dallas and driving over with her brother Frank. The trip will give them time to do some scheming before they get here."

"Guess we'll have to vacate our rooms then," said Granger.

"Oh, no. Don't bother. The kids can use the other two bedrooms. No need to switch around just for them."

"Are you sure, Phyllis?" insisted Teresa. "You know, our AC should be fixed today, and we've already taken such advantage of your hospitality."

"I'm very sure. I've never had such an exciting week. Why, not only have I come to appreciate this house and the ghosts I share it with, but I've also turned into a passable detective, even if I do say so myself. Besides, you guys are such great company. Good practice of my hosting skills for the party."

"Oh, yes. The party," repeated Teresa.

"It's on Saturday night. All the invitations went out three weeks ago, and I haven't received any 'regrets' so far. Guess all fifty people plan to come. Of course I know you guys didn't get a written invitation, but, as I said before, you're definitely invited. In fact, you're my guests of honor."

"Well, I don't know about that," said Jack.

"Yes you are," replied Phyllis, "my *esteemed* guests of honor."

"But we don't have much to wear," protested Teresa.

"Oh, whatever you have will be fine. It's not *that* formal."

They all finished eating, and Phyllis went into the kitchen to talk to Gloria and Charles.

"Well," asked Jack after Phyllis left, "what now?"

A rejuvenated Teresa said, "We should finish our job in the basement. Get it over with."

"Are you sure, dear?" asked Granger. "You weren't in very good shape last night."

"I feel much better now. I think I have my head on straight. Besides, it's daytime and the sun's out."

"It's bright out there all right," confirmed Jack. "Not a cloud in the sky when I looked outside through the kitchen window this morning."

"Say, was Charles out there then?" asked Granger.

"Come to think of it, I saw him over by the sheds and the garage."

"He was in the outbuildings?"

"Yes."

"What about the one with the entrance to the tunnel?"

"Uh...yeah, I guess I saw him go into that one too. In fact, now that you mention it, I recall thinking he was in there for a pretty long time."

"Umm." Granger sat and stared pensively.

"What is it?" asked Teresa.

"I...I think we better check the basement."

Teresa grunted. "You think Charles discovered the trunk we opened?"

"Maybe," said Granger.

They all leaped up out of their chairs simultaneously, called for Phyllis, and carefully descended the narrow steps with flashlights blaring.

"Well, the stuff is still here," said Granger as they surveyed the area where they had unloaded the trunk the night before. "Still all piled up on the floor."

"And there's more in the trunk we haven't examined. But, how do we know nothing is missing?" asked Teresa.

"We'll go through everything again," replied Granger.

They examined all the things that had been left there. Teresa could not bring herself to touch the blue dress, but it was still in the stack of clothes they had placed next to the trunk, and the trunk lid was still closed. Just then Phyllis climbed down from the top of the stairs.

"Phyllis, we thought Charles might have discovered the trunk this morning, so we came down to make sure everything is still here," said Teresa.

"Well?" asked Phyllis.

"As far as we can tell, it's all here, except the diary, of course."

"The diary? Where's that?" asked Jack.

"I have it upstairs in the bedroom," Teresa replied. "Charles doesn't even know there *is* a diary, so it should be safe."

"Are we ready to re-open the trunk now?" asked Granger.

"I suppose," said Teresa. She was starting to feel nervous again as she wondered what other surprises the trunk might hold.

Granger and Jack pushed the lid open and focused the beams of their flashlights inside.

"Mostly empty now," said Granger as he lifted one of the remaining items out of the darkness. He untied a knot in a ribbon and unfolded the thin paper that the ribbon held together. "Look. Here are some braids and hairpins. They have intricate carvings on them. Probably made out of bone."

"They're beautiful," said Phyllis. "I remember my grandmother had some that looked a lot like these."

"Ahh, and a lock of hair. It's auburn," said Granger. He held the piece, secured by a small white ribbon, between his thumb and forefinger. "Probably Sarah's hair."

"Yeah," agreed Teresa. She took the lock from Granger and lovingly brushed it with her fingers. "Soft and naturally curly." Then she put it back inside the paper with the other things.

"More books," said Jack as he lifted out five heavy volumes. "Sarah must have been a prolific reader." He stacked them next to the Dickens novels they had already found.

"Guess we have to keep in mind they didn't have TV or CD players back then," said Granger.

"Sheet music," reported Jack. He held up three sheets of lined paper with notes but no title. "Can anybody read music?"

"I can play the piano a little," said Phyllis. She scanned the notes and tried to hum the tune. "Sounds like some sort of minstrel song."

"Maybe Sarah could play too," said Teresa.

Granger peered back down into the trunk. It was empty.

"That's all," he reported.

"Nothing else? You sure?" asked Phyllis as she examined the inside with the beam of her flashlight.

Teresa pushed on the wood that formed the floor of the trunk. "Wait. This feels like a false bottom."

"Huh? You mean there's a compartment below it?" asked Phyllis.

"I think so." Teresa pressed on one side. "See. It moves. Help me pry it up at the edges."

"Wait," said Phyllis. "Here's a coat hanger you can use."

Teresa wedged the stiff wire into one corner while Granger pushed on the opposite side. The edge tilted up. Then Teresa curled her fingers around it and pulled. The bottom popped up revealing another small compartment below.

"See. It *was* a false bottom."

They all shone their lights down into the darkness.

"Wow," said Phyllis.

"My God," agreed Jack. "There it is."

"It's a leather bag, just like you saw in your vision, dear," said Granger.

"Umm," confirmed Teresa. Her hands were trembling again. She touched the supple leather and shook. The contents jingled. "Sounds like coins inside."

Granger and Jack pulled the heavy sack from the depths of the trunk and dropped it with a loud clanging thud onto the floor. Then they untied the knot that held it closed and poured the contents onto the floor.

"Gold coins. Lots of them," Teresa said almost breathlessly.

They all stared at the gleaming heap with mouths wide open.

"I don't know what to say," exclaimed Phyllis. "All these coins down here for over a century. Why, they look as if they've just been polished."

Jack picked up some of the pieces and tilted them back and forth in the beam of light from his lantern. "Say, these are Double Eagles. Looks like they're brand new."

"You know much about these things?" asked Granger.

"A little bit. It was my hobby when I was a kid. You know, the San Francisco mint and all. My dad used to take me to a lot of lectures and exhibits about gold coins." He examined some of them more closely, and his eyes widened. "Hey, there are some 1854-O's in here. Most of these things were minted in 1850 or 1851, but," he hesitated and counted silently, "I see at least ten...no twelve...1854 Double Eagles from the New Orleans mint. You know how *rare* these things are? Only about 3,000 of these babies were ever made, and less than ten uncirculated ones are known to exist...that is, until now."

"How much would the 1854's be worth?" asked Granger.

Jack was hesitant. "Hard to say, but a lot! And then there's the value of the others in here. Must be almost a hundred in all. This little bag could be worth an incredible amount of money."

Phyllis swallowed and ran her tongue across her dry lips. "I...I probably should sit down," she stammered as she grabbed Teresa's arm.

"Say, maybe this is what Charles has been looking for," said Granger.

"But, how would he know about the coins?" asked Jack.

"Well, he's a Bollinger. Maybe information about the coins was kind of passed down through the generations."

"Maybe," agreed Phyllis as she finally released her grip on Teresa's arm. "Then I guess, if that's right, the money would really belong to him and his kin." A slight smile grew across her face.

"Probably," said Jack. "Of course, I don't know the legalities. It's kind of a strange situation."

"So, now what?" asked Phyllis.

"I suggest we put all the stuff back in the trunk for now, including the coins, offered Teresa. "We don't know exactly what to do at this point, and it's all been here for almost a hundred fifty years. Can you think of a safer place—at least until we figure something out?"

"I suppose you're right," Phyllis replied.

"I'd like to take a few of the coins, if you don't mind, so that we can get them appraised. I know a dealer I can call," said Jack.

"Okay," said Phyllis.

"Yeah. That's probably a good idea," said Teresa. Deep down, she really did not want *anything* removed, but Jack's request made sense.

They placed all the treasures back in the trunk as closely as possible to the way they found them, including the bag of coins below the false bottom.

As they were finishing, Jack advised, "We should all keep our knowledge of the trunk and its contents, *especially* the coins, to ourselves. Other people besides Charles might be interested in helping themselves."

"Absolutely," agreed Granger.

"Of course," said Phyllis.

Teresa smiled. "Yes. That goes without saying."

They all stood looking at the filled trunk.

"Guess we're ready to close the lid," said Jack.

Suddenly, Teresa blurted out, "There's something else—another piece that belongs in the trunk."

"What?" asked Phyllis as she searched the area with her flashlight. "I think we've put it all back in, except for the few coins that Jack has."

"No, it's not the coins. It's something metal all right, but not coins."

"What is it?" asked Granger.

"I don't know…I…"

"Well, dear," said Granger, "we've put everything back in. There isn't anything else." He looked at Jack and continued, "Let's shut it."

Teresa closed her eyes tightly and turned away. With that, the men lowered the lid, and Phyllis locked it. Then they replaced the boxes and barrels to mask the path to the trunk, and they climbed back up the narrow staircase.

Chapter Nineteen

Later, after freshening up, they sat down for lunch in the dining room where Gloria had prepared a buffet.

"Oh, this iced tea tastes so good," said Teresa. "I think I was dehydrated."

"Sun tea," said Phyllis. "Gloria uses filtered water and steeps the tea on the back porch. It takes longer, but it sure does taste better." She stopped, looked around the table, and yelled toward the kitchen, "Where's the pickles, Gloria? You know I like those dills."

"Yes, ma'am," Gloria called back. "I'll bring 'em."

Charles entered the room and said to Phyllis, "Mrs. Runyon, I have some personal business to attend to this afternoon—that is, if you don't have anything pressing for me to do. Gloria said she'd handle my upstairs duties."

"Will you be back at all today?" Phyllis asked.

"Yes. Later, around dinner time."

"That's fine, Charles. We'll see you then."

After Charles left and Gloria went upstairs, Granger asked, "What about Charles? What are we going to do about *him*? We can't just leave everything down there sort of unguarded."

"Especially the coins," added Jack.

"He hasn't shown his hand yet," said Teresa, "Besides, the stuff is all locked up."

Granger continued, "Okay, but this mystery is getting curiouser and curiouser, as they say. I know we've learned a lot, but I'm not sure how much closer we are to figuring it all out."

"Oh, we're getting pretty close," said Teresa. "Don't worry."

Teresa knew that the mystery wouldn't be resolved until the all the puzzle pieces were exactly aligned, until the tension reached some critical level, until all the emotion and spiritual energy that had been building for a century and a half were at a maximum. Yes, she thought, the situation had to be similar to the original, such as it was during that long-ago party. Of course, it was so clear to her now—at the party.

******

"Gordon?"
"Yes, this is Gordon Carlson."
"Gordon, this is Jack McAlester."
"Oh, Jack. Didn't recognize your voice. How are you doing?"
"I'm doing great. Uh...are you sitting down?"
"Yeah. Why?"
"Well, you're about to feel pretty good too."
"Huh?"
"Gordon, I've just made what could be the greatest gold coin discovery of the last half century, maybe longer. I know where there's a bag full of almost uncirculated Double Eagles from the 1850s and, get this: There are several, like a dozen or so, 1854-Os in the lot."
"What?"
"Yep. The bag has maybe a hundred coins in it in all, some 1850s and 1851s, and it's been stored away in a trunk for a century and a half."
"Where in the world?"
"Let's just say I'm a long way from San Francisco."
"What do you want me to do?...that is, besides trying to slow my heart rate down."
"Well, nothing right now except start making some discreet inquiries to determine what a buyer might be willing to pay. Oh, by the way, what *is* the going price on 1854-Os like these?"
"I'll have to do some checking, of course, but the last good About Uncirculated 1854-O I saw on the market went for $235,000. If you want me to handle the sale, I'd have to figure out whether it'd be better to sell each individually or as a lot."
"Good. And keep in mind there's enough money in this thing for the both of us. You'd do well to get as high a price as possible for these babies."

"To give you a decent estimate for the whole lot, I'd need an inventory. I'd trust you to give me a good idea of quality, so as soon as you can get me that list...."

"Okay, okay, but I'm not in a position to do that right now. I'll let you know. Oh, and if you want to have any chance at all of handling the sale of any of these coins, keep this news under your hat. You understand?"

"Of course. No problem. In the meantime, I'll check the price for the 1850 and 1851 coins as well. Thanks for calling."

"I appreciate your input. Talk to you later. Bye."

******

Staring at her face in her bathroom mirror, Teresa traced the creases across her forehead and the crow's-feet extending from the corners of her eyes. She was starting to look really old. How could Granger or Jack be attracted to such an aging face? She stood back away from the mirror. "Chunky," she mouthed.

As she sat alone in the desk chair, she saw Sarah's small red diary within reach on the desk next to her. She stared at it for a moment and absentmindedly picked it up. She ran her fingers along the edges of the pages, pursed her lips and blew a puff of air, causing a small cloud of dust to rain down onto the desktop. She passed her hand through the cloud and rubbed her forefinger with her thumb.

******

"But, Mother, what do you have against Lance?" Sarah pleaded.
"He's not right for you," Vivian answered.
"Why, Mother?"
"He's too old, and he's a gambler, and...," Vivian hestitated.
"What else?"
"Well, he...uh...I blush to say it...he frequents dens of iniquity."
"Dens of iniquity?"
"Yes, he has dalliances with," lowering her voice to a whisper, "...ladies of the evening." Then, loudly, "*Completely* improper!"
"Oh, Mother. He loves me. He's told me so many times."
"He's after your money. That's what he loves."
"That's just not true."

"I forbid you to see him again."

"But he says he's coming to our party."

"He can't. He doesn't have time to get here from San Francisco."

"No, no. He's in New Orleans. He'll be coming from New Orleans. In fact, I received a letter from him last week. He said he was leaving that day and would arrive tomorrow, on the ninth."

Vivian was stunned. "Tomorrow? From New Orleans?"

"Yes." Tears streamed down Sarah's face.

With that, Vivian stormed out the door and slammed it behind her.

******

Teresa flipped through the pages of the old journal. As she turned the faded brown sheets, a coin dropped into her lap. It was a large penny, about the size of a present-day quarter. She looked at the date: 1821. Then she placed it back in the indentation from which it had fallen, and she turned the page:

Tuesday, January 2, 1855

Today was cold, very cold. The rain and sleet have been falling for several days now. I received a letter from Lance saying he will be coming to the party next week. He was at the St. Charles in New Orleans, where he always stays. I wrote him back that I look forward to seeing him, and I confessed my love once again. Of course he probably will not receive the letter before he leaves. I'm still trying to keep it all from Mother, but I know she suspects.

Wednesday, January 3, 1855

There was a slight break in the weather today, cold but sunny. I thought today about all those letters I sent to San Francisco when Lance was in New Orleans all along. I wonder what will happen to them. I suppose someone will hold them until they can be delivered at the appropriate time. I received another letter from him today. He was up river, near Bon Sejour, and he says he is bringing gifts with him. He wants to marry me, and I will do it no matter what Mother says.

Thursday, January 4, 1855

Mother says I can wear my new blue satin dress to the party next week. I am overjoyed because Lance will love it. I told Robert, in confidence, that Lance and I will marry, and he was not as happy as I expected. He has helped me correspond with Lance before, so I don't understand the change in his attitude. I played the piano today for almost an hour before Carrie came in to fetch me for my bath.

Teresa stopped reading and placed the book back down on the desk. She thought how prophetic Sarah's words were: "...until they can be delivered at the appropriate time". She smiled painfully. The words were so personal, so deeply revealing, that she just couldn't bear any more of it. She walked downstairs to find Granger and Phyllis still sitting in the parlor chatting away. Without disturbing them, she continued through the kitchen, onto the back porch and out the door. Soon she wandered into the flower garden, where she found Jack sitting on the bench.

"Well, well," said Jack, "taking another tour?"
"I guess. What are you doing out here?"
"I decided to come out to see the garden you and Granger liked so much."
"So, what do you think?" she asked.
"Nice, very nice. I wonder who's got the green thumb around here."
"Phyllis said there's a gardener who comes once a week, but I understand Charles likes to putter around out here when he's not busy doing other things."
She sat down next to Jack. "Jack, I know this may not be the right time or place...."

"Teresa, I know this experience has been hard on you, probably much worse than for any of the rest of us." He hesitated a moment. "But, I can take you away from all of this. I have a plan. We could be gone today...right now if you like." He took arm and pulled her against his chest.

"Jack, please." She tried to resist by pushing her hand against his shoulder.

He thrust his lips against hers and kissed her. She moaned softly, and then pulled away. Breathlessly, she said, "This is no good. We can't."

Jack cut her off. "I'm not finished. I...I'm supposed to return to San Francisco on Sunday. My wife, my secretary, everyone expects me then. But, Teresa, I'm ready to give it all up...everything...for you."

"It's not you, Jack. It's someone else who wants me."

He backed away.

"After reading some of Sarah's diary, I'm more convinced than ever of my direct connection with her...and you. It makes absolutely no sense, but I'm certain nevertheless."

"That's crazy," he said dismissively as he stood up.

Teresa grabbed his hand. "If it'll make you feel any better, I think this will all be resolved by Saturday night."

"Saturday night? Why?"

"Sarah and Lance were planning to get married against her mother's wishes. I think she was going to run away with him. This whole thing is building to some sort of climax, Jack, and I think the party here Saturday night is when it's going to happen."

"That's good," He hesitated for a moment. "...isn't it?"

"I think so." Then, as if she needed to convince herself, she repeated, "I think so." Despite these words, Teresa had her doubts. She harbored a fear of what Saturday night might bring, and she sensed that Jack might do almost anything to get his way.

Chapter Twenty

"Hello, Carol."

"Well, stranger, long time no hear."

"Yeah, yeah. How's everything going?"

"Well, so far your little alibis are holding, but I don't know for how long. Mr. Todd has been asking for you."

"What did you tell him?"

"I told him what you told me: you're in Houston at a business meeting and you'll be out of the office all week."

Jack fidgeted with the keys in his pocket. "Yes. That's good. Anything else?"

"Well, your wife called."

"Linda?"

"Yes, *that* wife."

"Uh...what did *she* want?"

"She wanted to know why you didn't have your cell phone on."

"Oh, that. Well, I've been in meetings."

"And she wanted to know why I didn't know where you're staying so she could call you there. She's about ready to ask the cops to put out an APB on you. And, I might add, so am I."

"Yeah, well."

"What the hell is going on, Jack? You're being way too mysterious about this trip. Have you gone off the deep end?"

"Carol, just stay with me on this."

"Well...."

Impatiently, he barked, "How many times have I saved *your* bacon by lending you a few extra bucks or letting you go home early or come in late?"

"Quite a few times, I guess." The phone was dead for a few moments. Then, in a soft voice, "Well, okay." Louder, she warned, "Until Monday, but that's *it*. After that, all bets are off."

"Great. Thanks, Carol. You're a doll."

"Yeah, yeah. It's getting deep in here."

"Bye."

He turned off the phone and thrust it into his pocket. Jack knew he really should call Linda, but, for some reason, he couldn't bring himself to dial her number. As vulnerable as he was, he didn't want to risk her wrath right now. He knew, in this case, his sanity, or what was left of it, would clearly be served best with a large portion of discretion.

******

Charles returned by the time they all gathered for dinner. They were more subdued than usual, each lost in his own thoughts. For a long while they sat without saying much of anything at all.

"Phyllis, you can tell Gloria she's prepared yet another fine meal," said Granger.

"Thanks. Gloria's a wonderful cook." When Gloria entered the room, Phyllis said, "Gloria, did you hear? Mr. Walker was congratulating you for a great meal."

"Oh, thank you, sir," Gloria said. "I fried the chicken, but Charles helped too. In fact, he baked the lemon pie you're going to have for dessert."

"Well, it's all been good, so I expect the pie will be too. Please ask Charles to come in so I can congratulate him as well," said Granger.

"Oh, he's not in the kitchen right now," replied Gloria.

"Where is he?" asked Phyllis.

"He's upstairs. He said he had to finish some work, so he went up there soon as the pie came out of the oven."

"Upstairs?" queried Teresa.

"Yes ma'am."

Teresa glanced at one person after another, stopping at Granger. "Uh, I think we need to run up to our bedroom for a minute."

"Huh?" Granger was biting a golden brown mouthful off the drumstick.

"Upstairs, dear. To the bedroom."

Granger swallowed. He could see the urgency in her eyes. "Oh, yes. The bedroom. Excuse us, please. We'll be right back...I think."

"What's going on?" asked Jack as they both bolted from the table toward the stairs.

"Beats me," replied Phyllis. "Maybe they had a sudden urge." She winked at Jack, and they both laughed.

Teresa ran ahead of Granger directly to the desk in their bedroom.

"Granger, did you take Sarah's diary? I left it here on the desk, and now it's gone."

"No. I haven't even been up here since lunch. Remember, Phyllis and I talked for a long time in the parlor."

"I should've hidden it somewhere. Now it's been stolen."

"Stolen?"

"Yes. Charles took it, don't you see? He knew we'd been in the basement, so he came up here and snooped around."

"Where *is* Charles? I thought Gloria said he was upstairs somewhere."

"I don't know. Didn't see him in the hall."

They abandoned their search after they failed to find him in the rooms upstairs. When they re-entered the dining room, Jack and Phyllis were just finishing the main course, and Gloria was serving lightly browned wedges of lemon meringue pie.

"You're just in time for pie," said Phyllis.

"Uh...yeah. That sounds good," replied Granger.

"How'd it go upstairs?" asked Phyllis.

"Oh, fine," replied Teresa.

They sat down and picked absentmindedly at the pie.

"Is it okay?" asked Phyllis.

"It's great," said Granger. He took a big bite, smiled and then nodded his head at Phyllis.

Picking up the hint, Phyllis ordered, "Gloria, why don't you get started cleaning up the kitchen, and ask Charles to help you."

"Yes ma'am, but I don't know where he is."

"Oh? Well, I guess you'll have to do it yourself."

"Yes ma'am". She left and closed the door to the kitchen.

Phyllis immediately turned to Granger and Teresa. "All right. She's gone. What's going on? I can see that something's happened."

"Well, I inadvertently left Sarah's diary on the bedroom desk," Teresa blurted out, "and now it's gone. I think Charles stole it. We checked everywhere upstairs, but we couldn't find him."

"But we would've seen him come by, wouldn't we?" asked Jack.

"Not necessarily," replied Phyllis. "There's another way from the foyer to the pantry and from there into the kitchen: a door, of sorts. I think it was designed to allow children to get from their upstairs bedrooms into the kitchen without being seen when adults were entertaining. You know: 'children should be neither seen *nor* heard'. Come with me. I'll show you."

Phyllis led them to the back of the foyer. She ran her hand along the wall and pushed at the seam where two large oak panels met. One of them gave way into the pantry on the other side.

"See. Someone can go through here to the pantry and into the kitchen."

"I suppose that's how he could've gotten past without our seeing him," said Jack.

"So where is he now?" asked Granger. He looked out the window. "His car is still out back."

"No telling," Teresa replied. "He could be in one of the outbuildings or even in the basement. In any case, he's probably reading the diary right now." She couldn't forgive herself for leaving the diary out where Charles, or anyone for that matter, could pick it up. She had been so solicitous of all the things they'd found in the trunk, *except* the diary. Of all the personal items locked away in that haunting time capsule in the basement, the diary was probably the most precious, more valuable in Teresa's estimation than the dozens of rare Double Eagles.

"Let's *all* look for him," suggested Jack.

"Okay," Granger responded. "Jack, you take the basement, Teresa and I will go out back, and Phyllis can handle the rest of the house. Oh, Phyllis, I suggest you make up some excuse to have Gloria leave for the day. We don't want to have to explain what's going on, at least not yet."

"Of course," she replied.

Within a few minutes they reconvened in the dining room.

"No sign of him in the house," said Phyllis.

"Nothing outside either," Teresa added.

Jack shrugged. "Well, it's awfully dark down in that basement. I looked as carefully as I could, and there was no sign of him. But you'll never guess what I *did* find down there in the tunnel. Don't know how we could've overlooked it before."

Teresa interrupted. "A large 1821 penny."

Jack's eyes popped open wide. "How'd you know? If this is another clairvoyant episode..."

Teresa shook her head. "It has nothing to do with that. There was an 1821 penny between the pages of the diary. So now we have proof he was down in the tunnel after he stole the diary."

"Yes," acknowledged Jack. "But we have no idea where he is now."

Teresa dropped her head and said sheepishly, "I think I'll just go to the bedroom and lie down."

"Are you okay?" asked Phyllis.

"Oh, I'll be all right...eventually. This is all my fault. I just need some time."

"You want me to come too, dear?" asked Granger.

"No. I'd like to be alone right now. I'll be down later."

"Okay. Just let me know if you need anything."

"Yes, please, if you want some tea or something," said Phyllis.

"Thanks. But, later...I'll be down later to have some tea."

Teresa squeezed Granger's hand and walked slowly up the grand staircase out of their sight. She lay on the bed for a while staring up at the ceiling. As she listened to the barely audible garbled phrases that drifted up the stairs and down the hall to her bedroom, she mentally rebuked herself for her mistake. Finally, exhaustion overtook her thoughts, and she closed her eyes and very soon fell asleep.

******

"Why, Lance, you're so naughty," Sarah scolded. "You've only just arrived and already you're tryin' to steal a kiss."

She turned her head so that he couldn't reach her lips. As she looked at Lance, she thought how handsome he was. Tall, muscular and impeccably dressed, he looked at her with large, deep-set coal-black eyes. His stare was mesmerizing, his touch strong and authoritative, not at all like the impotent gropings of the local young men of breeding her mother favored. The flecks of gray at the temples in his otherwise dark mass of hair denoted wisdom, making him all the more attractive. To Sarah, Lance Feldcamp was like her lost father, the personification of steadfastness, experience and maturity, qualities she most desired in a husband, and she was determined to have him.

Cold and shivering in a light rain, Sarah was leaning up against the wall of one of the outbuildings. She stole a quick look around the corner, at the back of the house.

"Now we have to be very careful. Mother could be watching."

"Don't worry," said Lance. "Your mother is upstairs taking a nap."

"How do you know?"

"Robert told me."

"Why, Robert is such a dear." She thought for a moment. "But, you know, I'm surprised he told you where she is. He hasn't been so helpful lately. In fact, I think Mother's rantings about you are starting to wear him down."

"Oh, I think he'll be more cooperative now," said Lance.

She frowned. "What do you mean?"

"I wrote you that I was bringing a present."

"For *me*?"

"Well, no dear, not *all* for you."

"Oh." She frowned again and pulled her coat tighter. "For whom, then?"

"One is for Robert—sort of a gift for helping to arrange our meetings. You know."

"What is it?"

"Oh, let's just say it's something Robert wanted and, indeed, *needed* very much—in fact, so much that I think he'll be even more cooperative now."

"But, Lance, what did you bring him?"

"I'll let Robert tell you. It's his now, not mine." He took a deep breath. "Now, let's make plans for our get-away."

Sarah giggled and averted her eyes. "Yes, let's."

"I'll have a carriage with a driver waiting for us down by the cemetery about ten o'clock the night of the party. By that time everyone, including your mother, will be so busy they won't notice we're gone. You just have to meet me there. We'll be off to New Orleans and, later, San Francisco."

"Yes—the night of the party. What a wonderful diversion! You're so clever, Lance. None of the juveniles around here could've come up with such an ingenious plan." She batted her eyes. "I can't wait." While embracing him tightly, she planted a long kiss on his lips.

Chapter Twenty-One

Teresa's eyes popped open, and she lay motionless. What did Lance give to Robert? Did Teresa and Lance follow through with their meeting? Where were Charles and the diary? How could she get the diary back? Her mind was racing.

"Sarah and Lance arranged to run away together the night of the party," said Teresa as she sipped on a hot cup of tea in the parlor. "She was wearing the blue dress that night, and that's when she was murdered."

"So she was killed at the party," concluded Phyllis.

"Well, maybe...maybe not. All I know is she was killed the evening of the party, when she was wearing the dress and when she and Lance had arranged to elope."

"Quite an intrigue," said Jack.

"Yes it was." Teresa swallowed another steaming mouthful and cradled the warm cup in her cold hands.

"Do you feel better now that you've had some tea?" asked Granger.

"A little bit. I can't explain it, but I have a new feeling...a fear really."

Granger frowned. "A fear?"

"I'm afraid of how this is all going to end...I mean with us here."

"Well, it's going to end by our finding out who murdered Sarah. Then all these visions of yours will stop and, after that, we'll pack up and go home," said Granger matter-of-factly. "And there's nothing to be afraid of. No one who lived a century and a half ago is going to hurt you or any of us."

"Oh, I'm not afraid of some ghost. That'd be silly. I'm frightened of someone living right now."

"Who?" asked Jack.

"That's the problem. I don't know. If I knew, then maybe I wouldn't be so afraid. I'd know what, that is *who*, to be on guard against."

"Look," said Granger, "there's absolutely no reason for your fear. We're all here with you. We don't know where Charles is, but he's really no threat as long as we're together. Right?"

Teresa responded slowly, "Right. But what if the person I should be afraid of *isn't* Charles?"

"Not Charles?" repeated Jack. "Who else could it be?"

"Teresa, you mean you're afraid of one of *us*?" asked Phyllis.

"No, no. Not really. I mean I'm just confused. This whole thing has been difficult for me."

"I understand. We *all* understand," said Phyllis as she took Teresa's right hand. "You're distraught. And who can blame you? You've been through a lot the last several days. You need to relax." As she sat back on the couch, a smile came across her face. "In fact, let's just forget about all of this tonight and do something silly…like play Monopoly. How about that?"

"Monopoly," said Jack. "I haven't played Monopoly for, oh, maybe twenty years."

Granger grinned. "That's a good idea, Phyllis. How about it, Teresa? You've always liked that game."

Teresa hesitated and then relented. "Okay, okay. Monopoly. But I have dibs on the shoe."

"Right. You get the shoe. I get the battleship," said Granger. "Okay, guys?"

"Well, I like the battleship too, but I'll settle for the iron," said Jack. "I know it sounds funny, but for some reason I like the iron. I think it's the token that gets the least respect."

Suddenly, they heard a sound out back. Phyllis went to the window and parted the curtains. "It's Charles. He's driving away in his car."

"Well, I wonder where he was hiding," commented Jack.

"I don't know, and I don't care. We're playing Monopoly." Phyllis turned away from the window to fetch the game board.

******

Friday morning dawned bright but steamy. Teresa felt secure as she and Granger lay awake in bed for a long time in each other's arms. He had strong arms, arms that had rejoiced with her during happy times and had supported her during times of crisis and despair, especially when the baby died. Because of her death, she would never know the joy of seeing a child of hers grow to adulthood. She would never be able to treasure experiences parents have always shared with their children: laughter at Christmas, pride in accomplishments, tears at times of disappointment or failure. Perhaps, if Granger had been more open to having another baby, she, like Phyllis, would be looking forward to seeing *her* children come home. Perhaps.

"I suppose Phyllis's husband and kids will arrive today," said Teresa as she stared at the ceiling above the bed.

"Yep. Things will be a bit noisier after they get here," Granger mused.

"It's been great with just the four of us for the last several days, but Phyllis is anxious to see her kids." Then, wistfully, "I know I'd feel the same way."

Granger didn't detect the nuance. "Oh, and it'll be nice to finally meet these people we've heard about." He looked around the room and frowned. "And the kids that put up all these darned posters."

They both laughed.

"You know, Phyllis told me the other day that her husband George is a business consultant of some sort who travels all over the world. She said he bought this house because he wanted to be near the lake. Evidently, he's quite a fisherman. Only he works so much he never gets to go fishing. Crazy, isn't it?" said Granger.

"It's crazy all right," she agreed. "Seems like people who can afford nice things never get to enjoy them, never get to pursue all the interests they have. I guess that's the very reason they can have nice things in the first place."

"It's a curse, I suppose—the way of the world."

******

Downstairs, Phyllis was on the phone with Charles, and Jack could tell she wasn't happy.

"I take it you...uh... talked to Charles," said Jack when Phyllis entered the room.

"Yes. We had what I'd call a *lively* conversation. He won't be back."

"Huh?"

"He quit."

"You mean just like that?"

"Yep."

"Did he say why, or did he tell you what happened yesterday?"

"Not really. He said he couldn't work here anymore."

"Charles quit?" asked Teresa as she and Granger entered the room and sat down on the couch.

"Yes," replied Phyllis.

Anxiously, Teresa continued, "What about the diary?"

"Oh, that. Well, he admitted taking it."

"But, the diary...where?" insisted Teresa.

"He said he left it near the trunk in the basement. He told me he didn't want 'the *thing*', as he called it."

"I'll go get it, dear" said Granger, and he immediately left to retrieve the book.

"Well, this is essentially his admission that he's a Bollinger," concluded Teresa. "What else did he say?"

"Not much. He said the house is depressing to him now. He told me it has 'negative history'."

"Hmm. Unusual term," Jack commented.

Granger returned with the diary and handed it to Teresa.

She thumbed through it. "It looks okay." She stopped suddenly. "Except the last few of pages have been torn out."

"Huh? Let me see," ordered Granger. He quickly flipped to the back. "Three pages are gone. I guess they held the entries for January 7th and January 8th." He looked back through the book again and added, "Wait. The entry for each day is no more than a page long, so why would he have torn out *three* pages? Why didn't he just tear out the two pages that had writing on them?"

"Maybe one of the entries was longer than a page," speculated Phyllis.

"Or he was in a big hurry and tore out a blank page by mistake," said Jack.

Teresa listened to their theories and then said, "*Or* the entries for the last two days took up only the usual one page each, and someone else wrote something on the last page."

"Huh?" Phyllis responded.

"You know. Maybe somebody added to the diary after Sarah's death...after the fact, as they say."

Granger was perplexed. "Well, I know we're all just theorizing, but, if I do say so, dear, your theory is pretty radical and..."

"Out of the box, Granger. Think out of the box," said Teresa.

"Well," Phyllis interjected, "we aren't going to solve this standing here. Let's have some breakfast. I thought we'd eat out on the porch. It's still cool enough that we won't bake, and it's our last morning before the crowd hits. After breakfast, I have to help Gloria with party plans. Now that Charles is gone, I'll have to take up the slack."

"Sounds good," said Granger.

They adjourned to the porch where a round glass-topped table with four wrought-iron chairs and a selection of light breakfast foods awaited them.

"It's actually very comfortable out here," said Jack.

"Yes. The old oaks shade the area, and the breeze keeps the porch cool. It's like this most mornings before the oppressive part of the day sets in."

"Say, Phyllis," asked Granger, "where does that stone pathway over there go?"

"Why, that's the old path to the cemetery."

"Ugh. Sorry I asked."

"Actually, that path was built by slaves, same as the original part of the house and the old outbuilding with the tunnel entrance," she said as she pointed. "It's always on the tours too."

"That's it," said Teresa.

"That's what?" asked Phyllis.

"It's the building Sarah was leaning against when she met secretly with Lance."

"Huh?"

"Oh, never mind."

"What about the other buildings and the trees?" asked Granger.

"Most of the other buildings date from the thirties. When we bought the place there was still a '37 Chevy decaying in the garage. The trees...well, who knows. Some of the big ones must've been around when the original house was built, even before Sarah's time. We know the trees along the fence line were planted in the thirties because we have a picture of a former owner planting them. The

Chevy was in the picture, so that dates it. In fact, I think the guy in the picture was a Bollinger.

"There isn't a small child in the picture, is there?" asked Teresa.

"As a matter of fact, there is. Funny you should ask," replied Phyllis.

"You know who that kid might be?"

"Uh..." Phyllis stammered.

"Charles...er...Craig Bollinger," said Teresa.

"*My* Charles?"

"Yep. The date would correspond to when he would've been maybe one or two years old, and the man planting the trees is probably his father Richard. The courthouse records said his parents died in the fifties. It all makes sense." Teresa smiled contentedly.

Granger's eyes widened. "Yeah, you're right, dear, it fits. I think you *are* Sherlock Holmes."

"So they were the last Bollingers to live here," concluded Teresa.

"I assume the Depression finally did them in, and they sold this place. I don't know what happened to them then," said Phyllis.

"I suppose they started a new life considerably lower on the food chain in the small house near the lake, the house Charles still lives in," explained Teresa.

Granger said excitedly, "Another piece of the puzzle just popped into place."

Jack added, "I guess I understand now why Charles would say this place has 'negative history'. But, if that's true, why did he want to come back to work here? And why the change in his attitude now?"

"Initially, he wanted to be back at his old home place. That's probably the reason he came to work here in the first place. But yesterday something changed," said Teresa. "He found out something, probably from the diary. Maybe there was some information on the pages he tore out, information that gave this place so much 'negative history' he couldn't bear to stay here." She thought for a moment. "But it would have to be devastating, much bigger than merely losing social status because his family went broke during the Depression. I mean, a lot of people lost everything then."

"You're right," said Granger. "And...if your theory is correct, it had to be a mortal blow, an absolutely crushing revelation."

Phyllis chewed the last morsel of toast that she had painted liberally with her precious raspberry jam. "Well," she said as she swallowed, "I have to be off to help Gloria with party preparations.

George called again this morning to tell me his plane was about to take off from Heathrow. So, he should be here by about eight tonight."

"What about your kids?" asked Jack.

"Oh, Frank called too. Julia is flying into Dallas about four. So, they should arrive by six. We probably won't wait dinner for George because he'll be up to his eyelids in jetlag. We'll wait for the kids, though, so plan on eating about seven. Just grub around in the kitchen for lunch. I'll be out of pocket all day. Okay?"

"That's fine," said Teresa. "We'll fend for ourselves."

"I'm going to check back with my coin dealer contact," said Jack. "And, if it's all right, I may go down and inventory all the Double Eagles."

"I can help you," volunteered Granger.

"I'll do some more diary research," said Teresa, "and I won't let it out of my sight this time."

"Great. Here's the key to the trunk. See you all later." With that, Phyllis disappeared inside the house.

Chapter Twenty-Two

Jack and Granger spread the Double Eagles across the dining room table. With no one around to see them, they acted like kids in a candy store. First they organized the 113 coins by mint year: 1850 to 1854. Then they subdivided the stacks based on Jack's judgment of the quality of each coin. After they finished, they counted thirteen of the valuable 1854-Os and 25 coins minted in each of the other four years.

"This is quite a haul," said Granger. "Why, I've never seen coins so beautiful. Now I can see why Midas had a gold fetish."

Jack agreed. "They don't make 'em like this anymore. Looking at this stash makes me wish I'd paid more attention at all those exhibits my dad used to take me to."

"Now what?"

"Well, now that we've made an inventory of the coins, I can call my dealer friend in San Francisco. He's been checking the pulse of the market for me. With the list we have now, he can give us a really good idea of a sales price for the whole lot."

"Unbelievable. I never thought I'd be involved in something like this."

After marveling at the treasure for some time, they placed all the coins back in the bag and locked it in the trunk once again.

******

Upstairs, Teresa sat in her bedroom staring at Sarah's diary as it lay on the desk. She knew it probably contained the answers to many of the questions she had about Sarah's motives and desires. It could even have enough evidence to tell her who murdered Sarah. But, inexplicably, she was finding it difficult to pick up the book. She was suddenly afraid she was so wrapped up in the events surrounding Sarah's death that she would be sad to see the mystery end. Actually, she could hardly remember what she had been doing before the visions started, and she was at a loss to think of anything as interesting to occupy her once the mystery was solved. After fighting these feelings for a while, she forced herself to pick up the diary and to start reading.

Friday, January 5, 1855

Lance arrived today, and I met him behind the smokehouse. Oh, he is so wonderful—handsome, dashing and strong. Mother did not see us, thank God, as she would have been furious. Lance gave me a fancy mirror and braids from that shop I like on Chartres Street. He said he had given Robert a gift as well, but he would not tell me what it is. Robert would not reveal it either. They are both being such rogues about it. Lance has a clever plan for us to elope Tuesday next during the party. He is so gallant.

Saturday, January 6, 1855

I confess that I stole away this afternoon to go on a carriage ride with Lance. We journeyed into town and sat by the river watching cargo being unloaded from the sternwheeler Southern Princess. We had such fun. I brought some food, which we ate on the way back. Unfortunately, Mother found out about my mischief and was very angry. I had to promise not to do it again, but of course my vow to Mother will not matter after Lance and I are married.

Teresa smiled as she read the words Sarah had penned so long ago. The timeless sentiments melted her heart and, once again, she found herself tearing up. She put down the book, stood up and stared out the window.

Across the wide yard and the pine forest beyond she could barely make out the dome of the Balfour water tower, recently repainted its familiar shiny silver. She smiled as she recalled Granger's tale of climbing the structure on a dare while he was in high school. Chuckling out loud, she reconstructed his story of gleeful victory after reaching the top and of utter embarrassment when he was caught in the act by the local constable. It was one of those high school rite of passage events he repeated all too often.

As she was about to turn away, her eyes caught the sudden glare of the late morning sun reflecting off the newly painted tower. She squinted and blinked. There was something familiar about the flash. She had had this experience recently, but *where, when*? She reopened her eyes, but the glare caused her to recoil again. All at once, she put the memory back together again in her mind. It had something to do with the trunk in the basement. The other thing that should be in the trunk: It was made of metal that reflected the light from Robert's lantern. What was it? She sat back down in the chair and reviewed the vision in her mind: Robert, the fabric, the bag of coins. What else? What could it be? She couldn't quite put her finger on it.

******

"Beautiful, isn't it, Mother?" asked Robert. He was sitting at the desk in the parlor pulling a shiny silver dagger out of an intricately carved leather scabbard.

"Yes, dear, it's nice," Vivian mumbled disinterestedly. She hardly looked, as she was busy shuffling papers and account ledgers. Suddenly she realized what he was holding and her attitude changed. "Where did you get that?"

"It was a gift, Mother."

"A gift? From whom?"

"Oh, a friend, just a friend."

"Must be a very rich friend."

"Yes, very rich. Actually, this isn't all he gave me."

"He? Who? And, pray tell, what *else* did he give you?"

"Can't reveal that. Let's just say it'll solve a lot of our problems."

"What?"

"Don't ask, Mother." Robert thrust the dagger back into its sheath and slipped it inside his belt. "I have to tend to some business now."

"Robert, you be careful with that weapon. Someone might try to steal it."

"Oh, don't worry about that. I can take care of myself."
He smiled at her and left through the front door.

******

A dagger—*that's* what it was. Teresa had seen the flash of light reflecting off the shiny blade of a dagger while Robert was at the trunk. She suddenly felt cold again, and she hurriedly walked downstairs.

"Granger...Jack," she called as she reached the bottom of the staircase.

She searched the parlor and dining room, but she couldn't find them.

Then, much louder, "*Guys, where are you?*"

She listened for a few moments, but she heard nothing. In fact, the place seemed to be utterly quiet, without even the usual house noises. She stood still and turned her head straining to hear something, *anything*, but there was nothing, not even the low, steady hum of the air conditioner or the chatter of birds outside. She detected no floor creaks or branches rustling in the breeze. The only sounds were the throb of her heart and the quickening sound of her breathing. It was *too* quiet—eerie, strange. As she stood in the foyer paralyzed, she closed her eyes. Then, suddenly, there was a loud slamming noise behind her. She jumped and shrieked.

"Teresa!" yelled Granger. "What's wrong?" He and Jack were coming out of the small door to the basement.

She thrust her hand against her chest as she realized what was happening. "Oh! You...you guys almost gave me a heart attack." She felt the throbbing inside her chest. Still frozen, she reached out for Granger and relaxed in his arms.

"Are you all right?" he asked.

"I called, but you didn't answer," she blurted out between breaths.

"We were in the basement putting the bag of coins back into the trunk," said Jack. "It's hard to hear down there."

"Yeah, well," she responded. Granger led her to a chair in the parlor where she could sit down.

"Rest here a minute and catch your breath," he ordered.

Jack retrieved a glass of water from the kitchen. After Teresa took a couple of quick swallows, he asked, "What were you doing? We thought you were upstairs."

"I was but I came down to find you guys." She was gradually getting back to normal. "I read some more of the diary, and I know now what *wasn't* in the trunk."

"Huh? What do you mean?"

"I mean what we didn't find, but Robert put in."

"What?"

"A dagger. A silver dagger."

Jack blinked. "What?" he asked.

"A knife. A knife made of polished silver in a fancy leather scabbard. Robert received it as a gift—from Lance, I think."

"Wow. Well, that by itself would be a treasure," said Granger.

Jack frowned and added, "But how do we know it was still in the trunk? I mean, Robert or someone else could've removed it years and years ago."

"Yes, but…I have a feeling…"

"Uh-oh. Another one of your feelings," said Granger.

Now recomposed, Teresa frowned at him. "I've been right about everything so far, haven't I?"

"Yes," he confessed, "I guess you have."

"So, why would you doubt me now?"

Granger shrugged and asked, "So, if we accept your premise, who has the dagger now?"

"I wish I knew," answered Teresa. "For a few terrifying minutes a while ago, I thought I was going to find out sooner than I wanted to." She grinned at them, and they all chuckled.

"I guess we shouldn't be laughing about a thing like that," said Granger.

"No, actually, we shouldn't," she replied as she rolled her eyes.

"Charles must have it," said Jack.

Granger agreed, "Yeah, Charles."

"Maybe," she said.

"Maybe? Who else could it be?" Granger asked.

Teresa tilted her head. "Well, we've all been down there with the trunk open, so we've all had our chances."

"Come on, Teresa," said Jack, "Do you really think Granger or Phyllis or I would've taken the dagger?"

She slumped back in the chair. "No. Not really. I suppose I'm just being paranoid."

"Yes you *are*," confirmed Granger. "You need to lighten up a little bit. Remember, you're the one who said Charles would hang himself if we gave him enough rope. Well, I think he just did. You've proved your point, so you can back off now."

Teresa relented. "You're right. I said that, and you're probably correct. I think he's hanged himself too. So now all we have to do is get him to tell us where the dagger is."

Granger thought for a moment. "I suppose the dagger was the murder weapon."

"Yes. I don't think there's any doubt," she said.

"So why would Robert save it?" asked Jack.

"Maybe he wasn't *saving* it, maybe he was *hiding* it," she replied.

Jack frowned. "Why would he have done that if Lance was the killer?"

"Well, maybe Lance *wasn't* the killer."

Jack frowned. "Oh. So who was?"

"Could be a lot of people. Or maybe Lance *was* the killer, and Robert wanted to cover it up to make sure no one found the money."

"Wait. Explain the money," requested Jack.

"Well, I think Lance gave Robert *both* the dagger *and* the money."

"Why would he do that?" Granger asked.

"Lance wanted to marry Sarah, so the money was a bribe to guarantee Robert's support for the marriage. And the Bollingers weren't in great shape financially, and that was a lot of money back then. I guess you'd call such an arrangement a 'you scratch my back, I'll scratch yours' thing. Or maybe it could be called a reverse dowry."

"Umm. Convoluted," said Jack.

"Maybe you're right, dear," agreed Granger. "But it still doesn't conclusively tell us who the murderer was."

Teresa shook her head. "That's true, but at least we're getting closer all the time."

"Well, I'm in favor of whatever will get us to the end of this whole thing as soon as possible," said Granger. "I confess I'm having a hard time keeping up, especially with all these visions you keep having."

"Me too," said Jack.

"Well," said Teresa. "I think I've recuperated now. Let's go scrounge around the kitchen and see what we can find for lunch."

"Great. When in doubt, eat something. That's my motto," said Jack.

Granger smiled at Jack. "I'm going to start using that as my motto, too."

Chapter Twenty-Three

"Hello, Gordon?"

"Yes, Jack. I recognize your voice this time."

"Gordon, I have an inventory of the coins we found. Did you find out anything on your end?"

"I did indeed. Jack old boy, you're going to be a very happy man."

"So, give me some numbers."

"Well, as you know, there aren't any Uncirculated 1854 New Orleans Double Eagles known to be in existence ...at least up to now. If you have some, they could easily be sold for $300,000 each. About Uncirculated would draw approximately $275,000. The corresponding 1850s would sell for $12,000; 1851s, 1852s and 1853s for $10,000 each." He hesitated a moment, then added, "So...how many do you have?"

"Well, there were 113 total coins, thirteen of them 1854s. Now get this: *five* of the thirteen appear to be Uncirculated and the other eight are About Uncirculated. Then, there are twenty-five more dated each of the other four years. So, what's the total value on that?"

The phone was silent for a long time as Gordon calculated. "Well, if the values hold, the total is four and three-quarter million dollars." Silence again. "Almost five *million*, Jack."

Jack groped for words. "Yeah. Almost five million. Got it."

"So...uh...what are you going to do with the coins, Jack?"

Jack knew Gordon was salivating over the fat commission he could earn as the selling agent. It was the deal of a lifetime. Jack didn't dare even intimate that he was not the owner of the coins. "I...I don't know." His mind was reeling. Finally, he blurted out, "I'll have to call you, okay?"

"Sure, sure, Jack. Anytime. I'll be waiting to hear from you."

"Thanks for your help, Gordon. Bye."
"Of course. Bye."

Jack was blown away. He sat on the bed in his room lost in a blank stare. Five million dollars would make him an independently wealthy man. If he invested the money wisely, he could live comfortably for the rest of his life. He could provide for his children and could take or leave Linda. In fact, without Linda, the five million would go so much farther: no designer dresses, no shopping sprees for twenty new pairs of shoes at a time, no five hundred dollar hair days. He could take or leave his job, too. Financially, whether he succeeded in his quest for that office on the next floor would become moot. He could run away with Teresa, an adventure like those he dreamed about when he was lying on the beach during Spring Break. He would be at once rich and fancy-free, and he could afford to be as lascivious as he liked. The prospect was almost overwhelming.

Jack turned on the bed and unzipped his suitcase. He reached inside and opened a compartment that extended the length of the back spine. From deep within, he retrieved an ornate leather scabbard and held it, lovingly, in his hand. A grin grew across his face as he admired the suppleness of the skin, the uniform color of the tanned surface, and the wondrous aroma of the genuine material with which it was made. He caressed the hilt of the tool it contained. There, below the hilt, was the sleek, finely-made steel weapon. He very slowly pulled the dagger out of the scabbard and examined it. Exquisite. Not a nick on it. He wondered how much *it* might be worth. He admired the shining blade and read the words engraved in very small letters near the handle:

Toledo

España

This was a fine instrument, used only once, and no one need ever know its history. He touched the point to his index finger. Still razor sharp after all these years, the blade immediately sliced through his skin, causing a drop of blood to appear. Yes, it was quite dangerous, but it was also a work of art—beautifully curved and perfectly balanced, with a silky surface soft as melted butter, just like those tanned, long-legged girls at Malibu so many years ago.

******

Teresa and Granger decided to go by to their own house during the afternoon to check out the air conditioning and to collect clothes for the party. They drove the few miles on the winding two-lane road, wet because of a brief, sudden shower. The sun was out again, and the vapor rising in waves from the soft blacktop created a steamy fog that hugged the hot roadbed.

On the way back to the Bollinger mansion, Granger asked, "I hate to bring it up again, but what happens if this mystery isn't resolved by Saturday night? Jack plans to leave Sunday morning, and we have no reason to stay at Phyllis's house any longer now that our air conditioner is fixed."

"I don't think I need to answer that question. Everything will be clear by Sunday." Teresa exuded confidence.

"So, why is it taking so long to get this thing resolved? Why Saturday night?"

"I'm not sure. I think there's just a normal progression for everything. You know: a time to be born, a time to die...."

"Yeah, yeah. I'm familiar with the verse...and the song, too."

"You just can't rush these things. Events happen for a reason, you know."

Granger thought for a minute before he decided to take a risk. "Does that include the accident?" He pressed his lips together tightly after mouthing the last syllable and waited for Teresa's usual defensive response.

"Granger...." She stopped short and then said calmly, "Granger, you know, you're right. It does."

"Huh?"

She could see that he was flabbergasted. "Yes. There *is* a time for everything. I guess it was just *her* time."

"What do you mean?"

Teresa suddenly felt a warm rush of certainty welling up inside her. "Well, I know I've always looked at what happened to the baby as being so wrong—much, much too early for her to die. And, of course, it was, in our eyes. But, when you look at it a different way, maybe it really *wasn't* early at all. It was right in God's time. It was just her time to go." She looked at Granger. "You see?"

"Uh, yeah. I see. I think." He looked away from her, through the false fog, over the canopy of pines, toward the rolling hills in the distance. Then he pressed his lower lip between his teeth.

Teresa pursued the point. "So, there's a time when the mystery about Sarah will be solved. We just don't know exactly when that'll be. Only I think it'll happen very soon."

"But waiting is the hard part," he responded.

"Umm. Yes, but I can almost guarantee the wait will be worth it."

"What do you mean?" he asked.

"Just be patient, dear, just be patient." She hesitated, and then added, "The final act in this drama will shock us all."

They sat in pensive silence for several minutes. Then, while they were stopped at an intersection, Granger leaned over and kissed her.

******

As they entered the long driveway leading to the columned porch of the Bollinger mansion, they saw both Phyllis's car and another unfamiliar one parked near the garage.

"Granger and Teresa Walker, meet my son Frank and my daughter Julia," Phyllis said as she greeted them in the foyer with two young people beside her.

Granger grinned at the lanky young man with a heavy five-o'clock shadow standing before him. "My mother's told us a bit about the experiences she's had with you all and Mr. McAlester this week. Sounds wild," said Frank as he tossed back his mop of dark brown hair. Granger detected a reticence in his voice.

Julia smiled and extended her hand. "I wish I'd been here this week. Imagine. Real ghosts in the house the whole time we've lived here. It beats all." Granger was taken by her curly red hair and soft Southern accent.

"It's just wonderful to meet both of you," said Teresa. "We've heard a lot about you. I feel like I already know you. In fact, we've been sleeping in one of your bedrooms." Granger saw Teresa raise her eyebrows slightly, and his thoughts suddenly focused on the wild posters in the bedroom.

"Uh...Frank, I understand you're an architect," offered Granger.

"Why, yes. I'm at one of the larger Dallas firms. We mostly design those four- or five-story suburban office buildings."

"I guess you keep pretty busy," said Teresa.

"Oh, yes. But of course I'm doing mostly grunt work right now. The major partners get the good stuff."

"Well, it's all good experience," responded Granger.

"What about you, Julia?" asked Teresa.

"I'm in Med School at Tulane. I've been going to school for...well...a very long time. I know Mother and Dad are ready for me to be out, but I still have a couple of years to go, then residency somewhere. Seems like it never stops."

Phyllis was exuberant. "Oh, we're ready for her to be finished, but we're also very proud of her. She's always been interested in a medical career, and soon she'll be realizing her dream."

Granger noticed that Frank's eyes turned away toward the floor.

"Well, how's the AC, Granger?" asked Jack as he came down the stairs and introduced himself to Frank and Julia.

"Fine. It's working fine. We even had to turn it down a bit because it was freezing out the place."

Phyllis interjected, "Uh...well, let's all adjourn to the dining room. I think Gloria is going to have dinner ready soon."

"But what about Dad?" asked Julia.

"Oh, he won't be here until about eight at the earliest, so we aren't going to wait."

"Well, Mrs. Walker, you have quite a story," said Frank after they had all sat down at the table. "I believe you, but I confess that some of it is very difficult to take. I mean the ghosts, the visions."

"I know. I understand what you're saying, but I've had to come to terms with them because of my experiences this week. I never would've believed any of this stuff either if it all hadn't happened to me."

"Frank, if I may," said Jack, "I'd like to add something. I started out doubting too, but the things that have happened this week have totally convinced me. There's no question Teresa's been, for want of a better word, *seeing* events that occurred a hundred fifty years ago."

"I guess I don't have as much trouble as Frank believing you, Mrs. Walker," said Julia timidly. She looked directly at Phyllis. "I've never told anyone, including you, Mother, but one time when I was in high school, I heard something. It scared me to death, but I was afraid everyone would say I was crazy if I mentioned it. So, I didn't."

"What was it, honey?" asked Phyllis empathetically.

"I heard someone crying, sobbing really, in one of the old bedrooms."

Teresa's eyes opened wider. "You heard that?"

"Yes. Was that one of the ghosts?"

"We think it's Sarah's mother Vivian crying in her bedroom after Sarah was killed."

"Well, that would explain the other thing, which was even scarier."

Teresa inquired, "What other thing?"

"The girl, probably about my age at the time, in the old west bedroom late one night. I'd been up late studying and had gone downstairs to get some hot chocolate or something. When I walked back up the stairs past the west bedroom, I noticed a light shining under the closed door. So, I opened the door and looked in."

"What did you see, dear?" Phyllis reached across the table and touched Julia's hand.

"Well, it hadn't been long since I'd heard the crying. I saw a girl sitting at that small desk on the far side of the room. A candle was burning next to her, and it was the only light in the room. She was busy writing in some sort of book or journal, but suddenly she stopped...as if she'd heard me. When she turned her head directly toward me, I could see that her face was all cut up and she was bleeding. Hmm...gives me cold chills now, even after so many years. I slammed the door shut, ran to my room and covered my head with the blanket."

No one spoke for a few moments. Phyllis finally broke the awkward silence. "Well, Julia, that's a terrifying story. Why didn't you tell me about it back then?"

"As I said, I didn't want to sound like some hormone-imbalanced teenager. I thought you might send me to some doctor if I said anything."

"Now, dear, you know I love you too much to ever have..."

"Oh, Mother," said Frank, "don't be so melodramatic."

"Frank," Phyllis scolded.

"Anyway, Mrs. Walker," interrupted Julia, "I guess you can see why I'm more receptive to your story than Frank is."

"Yes, I can understand that," said Teresa. "Uh...you never heard or saw anything like that again?"

"No. Nothing, thank goodness. I might not have been able to stay here if I had."

"Well, I think that's enough about ghosts and such at the table tonight," said Phyllis as she swallowed a mouthful of rice. "Let's talk about the party."

"Yes, indeed, the party," agreed Julia. "I'm looking forward to it, Mother. We haven't had a good party here since my last high school soiree. Remember that one?"

"Of course, dear. It was right after graduation. There must've been fifty or sixty kids over here dancing, laughing, and generally having a good time. I think that party lasted until, oh, five in the morning. Then we had some breakfast."

"And after everybody left, we collapsed for the rest of the day. I think I finally crawled out of bed about four in the afternoon."

"I heard about that one," said Frank. "I was between semesters at SMU, but I didn't come home that time. I guess I didn't want to be associated with high school kids. Below my station, you know."

"Oh, Frank," protested Julia as she muffled a laugh.

"You all must have had some wonderful times in this house," said Granger.

"We did. I miss it very much sometimes," said Julia as she looked around the room. "It's a wonderful place...despite my...uh... experiences."

Chapter Twenty-Four

"Sorry about missing dinner, honey," said George to Phyllis as she helped him unload his luggage from the car. The tall, big-boned Mississippian with a warm drawl clutched his wife closely. She stretched on tiptoes to reach his wide shoulders and wrap her hands around his thick neck. "I just had to spend that last day with the boys over there. Almost got a deal wrapped up."

"Oh, that's okay. You couldn't help it," replied Phyllis as she looked longingly into his dark brown eyes. Suddenly she giggled.

"What?"

"Your hair." She touched the disheveled mass on his head and pushed it to one side.

"Oh. I slept on the plane. Guess I'm a mess."

"I missed you terribly, dear," she said as they walked back into the house.

"And I missed you too," he replied. "Boy, I'm tired. Guess the jetlag's got me. You know I'd have been much better off just staying in London through the weekend. I have meetings there again early next week."

"Now don't start," said Phyllis. "You have to be here for your own party."

"Well, actually it's *your* party, not mine, you know."

"Umm. Oh...before we go in the house, I should tell you that we found gold coins in the trunk, a whole bag full of them."

George's eyes widened and he pulled Phyllis to the side of the driveway.

"Coins? I can't believe it."

"Yes...there's probably a hundred gold coins—rare Double Eagles. And some are in mint condition."

"Well, what do you know. And after all these years, too. I guess some of those stories were true. We should have done a better job searching that basement long ago."

Phyllis could see that George's mind was reeling as he tried to comprehend the discovery. "Maybe. But I doubt we could have been successful without Teresa's help."

"What else did you find?"

"Just a bunch of old stuff from Sarah's time." She lowered her voice to a whisper. "But, here's the kicker: Teresa says something else was in the trunk."

"Huh? What do you mean 'something else'?"

"She says a dagger was originally hidden in the trunk, too. But we haven't found it."

"That's strange. So what does it mean?"

"Well...I don't really know."

"Are the coins are still in the basement?"

"Yes. Locked back in the trunk."

"Well, don't let on about anything, especially about me. We've kept it a secret this long. We can keep it until everybody clears out."

"Whatever you say. We'd better get on in the house."

******

After the introductions, they all sat in the parlor.

"Since Charles is now...uh...unavailable, I've hired another man to replace him," said Phyllis. "He comes highly recommended, and he'll be bringing two more servers he's worked with before to help tomorrow night. And, of course, Gloria will be here."

Teresa watched George carefully. Though she had just met him, she had a strange feeling about this bear of a man. His physical size was reason enough to notice him, but his expansive personality was, if anything, even more compelling. He always seemed to be smiling and stroking everyone in a down-home, glad-handing way, the type of guy who is always the life of the party. Still, there was something about him, something that made her think he wasn't exactly as advertised.

Finally Teresa said to George, "Granger and I want to thank you and Phyllis for letting us stay this week and inviting us to the party on such short notice. And I think Jack would say the same thing."

"Absolutely," agreed Jack.

George grinned broadly as he sipped water from his glass. "Well, from what Phyllis has told me, you all will be the topic of conversation tomorrow night. What's happened here this week has certainly piqued *my* interest, and I think our guests will be just as taken with it all." He scanned the room. "I've always loved this place, but now...well...I feel so much closer to its history and to the people who've lived here. And, without *you*, I wouldn't be saying that tonight." He hesitated for a moment and set his glass down. "Well, I need to excuse myself. The jetlag is really getting to me. I'm going to have a quick snack and turn in for the night. I'll see you all in the morning."

"Good night, dear," said Phyllis. "I'll be there directly."

Frank and Julia smiled and followed George out into the kitchen.

"I could tell he was exhausted," said Teresa.

"Yes. He's had a thirty-hour day," agreed Phyllis. She fidgeted for a minute, and then added, "Well, I need to go on to bed too. Big day tomorrow. I'll see you in the morning."

"Good night," said Jack.

Frank and Julia were just then coming back.

After Phyllis had disappeared up the stairs, Frank turned to Teresa. "Umm...well, we...that is, Julia and I would like to make a request." Teresa almost knew what was coming. "We'd like to ask that you *not* say anything at the party about this crazy mystery of yours."

"But your dad is sort of excited about telling people," said Teresa.

"I know, but we've talked to him, and he's agreed not to bring it up."

"But why?"

"It's, you know, kind of unusual...kind of on the fringe," said Frank. "We'd just like to keep it among us. That is, you all and our family. That way there won't be any questions." He looked directly at Teresa. "You *do* understand, don't you?"

"I suppose." Teresa really didn't understand, but she knew she was much too close to the mystery to be unprejudiced. She was consumed by it, and she totally believed in it. Frank, Julia and George had not been through what she had experienced during the week. How could they possibly be as invested as she in its outcome? How could they be convinced that it was real and not some incredible group delusion? "What do you want us to do...or *not* do?" she asked.

"Just don't mention it at the party or to anyone who might come to the party. Pretend you're all conventional houseguests...old friends who are visiting. You know what I mean?" replied Frank.

Teresa started to shake her head but quickly stopped. "Yes, I get it."

"Have you talked to your mother about this?" asked Jack.

"No. Not yet, but we will," said Julia. "She'll go along with whatever Dad wants to do."

******

"What do you think is going on with Frank and Julia?" asked Granger while he was climbing into bed.

"Oh, they just don't want the family to become a laughingstock," replied Teresa. "They're thinking about appearances. How would it look if the family became notorious for harboring ghosts? Wouldn't do much for George's career or for Frank's or Julia's either." She shrugged. "I guess I don't blame them, but it's hard for me to accept. At first I was sort of offended. But I've had time to think about it, and I'm okay now."

She slipped under the covers next to Granger.

"Well, I can see their point." He scratched his head and continued, "So...uh...if I might ask, what are we going to actually be *doing* during the party tomorrow night?"

"I don't know about *you*, dear, but I intend to have a good time," she replied. Teresa snuggled over close to Granger and smiled at him. "Say, what did you do with that uniform you were wearing the other night?"

Granger was puzzled. "I took it home when I went to get our clothes. Why?"

"Oh, I just thought you could put it to good use again tonight. You know, like *last* time." She winked, put her arm around him, and pulled his lips to hers.

"You can call on me anytime you like, my dear, in or out of uniform...especially *out*," replied Granger. He switched off the lamp on the nightstand and turned his attentions back to Teresa.

"Why, colonel," she drawled, "I wouldn't recognize you without your epaulets."

******

"The party is just wonderful," Sarah whispered in her mother's ear. She was breathless and almost giddy with joy. The cream of plantation aristocracy from miles around was in attendance. Even Uncle Sibley had made the journey upriver from Natchitoches.

"You're so lovely, my dear," said Uncle Sibley. He smiled enthusiastically from his seat next to Vivian. "That dress fits you perfectly." He knew his comment was self-congratulatory, but he couldn't help himself. "Why, even those old fuddy-duddies sitting across the room are taking notice." He was looking at several dowagers staring disapprovingly at Sarah. "I didn't know they still had enough life in them to notice *anything* anymore."

The small orchestra struck up a tune, and Sarah took the arm of a young man for the next dance. Just then she noticed Lance, formally dressed in long coat and tie, walking from the foyer into the parlor. She immediately excused herself and ran up to him. Grabbing his arm, she said in a loud whisper, "Lance, what are you doing here? I didn't think you'd actually come to the dance. I thought we were just meeting later."

"If we're to be married, Sarah, your mother has to acknowledge me. I'll not be an outcast before I'm even part of the family."

"But, Lance. It would be better if you didn't..."

He moved past her and walked up to Vivian.

"Mrs. Bollinger, so wonderful to see you again. I'm honored to have been invited to this elegant party."

Vivian bristled and barked contemptuously, "Mr. Feldcamp, I'm sure I don't know why you're here. You were *not* invited to this party."

The people sitting nearby, including Uncle Sibley, turned as they heard her words.

"I beg to differ with you, Mrs. Bollinger. I was indeed invited...by your daughter. As we are now betrothed, don't you think I *should* be present here tonight?"

"*Betrothed!* That's a lie, Mr. Feldcamp. Sarah is certainly *not* engaged to you. Neither her brother Robert nor I have given permission for Sarah to marry *anyone*."

He raised his finger as if to scold her. "Ah, yet another misunderstanding on your part, ma'am."

Sarah interrupted. "Lance, please. Don't make a scene."

Robert, who had been chatting with some cronies in the dining room, came into the parlor when he heard the voices. "May I be of some assistance, Mother?" he asked.

"Robert, please tell this...*person*...that he and Sarah are *not* engaged and escort him to the door."

He turned to Lance. "Mr. Feldcamp, if you would please honor my mother's request. This is, after all, her home."

"But she must recognize me as Sarah's future husband."

"*Don't say that!*" screamed Vivian. The music had stopped, and everyone was listening now.

Sarah pulled at Lance's jacket. "Lance, I beg you. *Please.*"

"Mr. Feldcamp, we can talk later about this matter." Robert's voice was strong and authoritative.

"Robert, I thought we had an understanding," protested Lance.

"*Later*," Robert reiterated. He placed his face directly in front of Lance's.

Relenting, Lance said, "Later then." He glared at Vivian. "Yes, later will do." Then he turned to leave the room.

"Lance!" cried Sarah. She wilted into Robert's arms and began sobbing.

Everyone stood open-mouthed as Lance left through the front door.

Vivian gritted her teeth, turned toward the orchestra and commanded, "Start the music again." Then she smiled, scanned the startled faces around the room. "Dance, please dance."

Chapter Twenty-Five

Not able to sleep, Teresa crept down the stairs and sat on the couch in the parlor. The mantle clock ticked in even monotonic rhythm, and a small lamp glowed only dimly. The room was quiet and comforting, almost totally insulating her from the rest of the world. Soon she was lost in thought, and she visualized the room as it must have appeared during that party so many years ago. That night the room was filled with giggly ingénues dancing with eager young bucks under the watchful eyes of their smiling mothers and solicitous fathers. How would she have felt if she had been there? Her mind wandered, careening back and forth between then and now, past and present, fantasy and reality. Certainly, as a woman, she would have been constrained by the rigid mores of the period. Life was less complex then, but she wondered whether the greater simplicity compensated for a lack of freedom. Did Sarah experience happiness as we know it now? Would she herself have been satisfied to live in Sarah's world? No, she thought. No way. Suddenly she was startled by a noise behind her.

"Well, well, up again," said Jack.

So much emotion had built up inside her that she was eager to talk to somebody, to anybody, who would listen. "I had another one of those dreams. It was about Sarah's party..."

Jack sat down next to her. "Teresa, I have something important to tell you."

"Huh?" Her attention was still hanging somewhere between the centuries.

Jack's voice was firm and clear. "We've known each other for less than a week now, but, as you yourself said, there's an attraction, a real connection, between you and me."

"Jack, I...." The fog was lifting, and she began to realize what was happening.

"Wait. Let me finish." He took a deep breath. "I've thought a lot about...well...*us*. You know I have a family, Teresa—a wife and two kids. I've tried to consider them, but...I've come to a decision." His eyes burned into hers.

"A decision? What do you mean?" She was clear-headed now, focused and aware.

"Teresa, I love you. I know it's crazy. I know it's wild, but think about it. We could just leave here, tonight. We could be on a plane to Mexico in the morning." He moved toward her, cradled her head in his hands and pressed his lips on hers. Then, nervously, "And we could have all the money we want to enjoy ourselves."

A thousand thoughts streamed through Teresa's mind. Was she a player reenacting some long-ago drama that had taken place in this very room? Her attraction to Jack was certainly seductive. But she remembered what Granger had told her: "I'm with you, and you're in the here and now. You're not some 'channel' from the past to the present. You're my wife, and you live in the *twenty-first* century, not in the nineteenth." The words screamed at her.

She knew what she had to say. "Jack...Jack...hold everything." She pushed him away. "Listen to me. I'm married to Granger. I love him and only him. And, most importantly, I live *now*, not a hundred fifty years ago, and that's *that*."

His head dropped, and, with desperation in his voice, he responded, "But, Teresa."

"Jack, you've become a very fast friend, and, believe me, I understand what you're going through. Heaven knows only you and I can *really* understand it, but there'll be nothing other than friendship between us. I'm staying with my husband, and you should go back to your wife and kids." She stood up and stared back at him. "That's just the way it is. I hope you can see the wisdom of what I've said."

All at once he felt a flood of anger, and he grabbed her arm. "Teresa, I'm not going to give up on you." She could see that his jaw was fixed.

"*Please*, Jack! Don't make me scream. I'll see you in the morning." She pulled away and walked slowly toward the foyer. She focused on reaching the stairs first, then up each step one at a time. She was afraid to stop, afraid to look back. Finally, once she was inside her bedroom, she locked the door and breathed a sigh of relief.

Jack sat on the couch struggling mightily with the devil inside him. Primitive emotions were boiling up, scalding his heart and devouring his soul.

******

Granger was in a good mood when he woke up. For some reason, he felt almost silly as he shaved. He thought about that loquacious trio of pubescent girls who used to drive him crazy in all his high school classes. They always seemed to be engaged in frenetic conversation about some boy or about the secret machinations of a rival clique. Because everyone was seated alphabetically, they sat near him, and they usually indignantly ignored his pleas for quiet. He smiled and chuckled under his breath as he remembered their antics.

"Penny for your thoughts," said Teresa as she staggered past him on her way to the shower.

"My thoughts aren't even worth a penny," he replied.

"Unfortunately, mine are," she said as she turned on the water.

Granger frowned. "What do you mean by that comment?" He could see that Teresa was hiding something.

"Oh, nothing." She didn't want to discuss what happened in the parlor the previous night. "I asked you first."

"Well, I was thinking about my high school classmates. You remember I told you about Dotty, Brenda Jo and Alice."

"You mean 'The Three'?"

He laughed. "Yeah. They went *everywhere* together, at least when they were at school. Always wondered if they were as inseparable away from campus. What do you think happened to them?"

"You never heard anything about them after graduation?"

"I never heard much of anything about *any* of my classmates after graduation, dear. High school was not my favorite period."

"I know, dear, but, if anyone from your class is here tonight, be nice to them."

Granger frowned. "Of course I'll be nice."

"Yeah, well, any wounds inflicted so long ago should've healed by now."

"Some wounds don't heal very quickly, some take a long time. You, of all people, should understand that."

"Hmm."

Granger knew he'd hit a nerve, so he backed off quickly. "Anyway," he said, "maybe I'll see *somebody* I know tonight."

******

Frank and Julia had risen very early and were about to leave the breakfast table when Granger and Teresa came downstairs. George and Phyllis had just sat down, and Jack was talking to Frank about their common interest in the consequences of excessive stress and strain on structural steel.

"Busy day today, Phyllis?" asked Granger.

"*Very* busy. Chris, the new butler, should be here within the hour with all his people. Gloria and I are going to do some decorating, and the caterers are coming in the afternoon to set up."

"Boy, you *are* going to be busy," said Teresa.

George was downing a plateful of scrambled eggs and two pieces of toast. "I'm going to be upstairs on the computer. I might as well get in as much work from here as I can."

Phyllis looked at him. "The main thing I'd like you to do is stay out of the way."

"Great. After finishing my work, I can watch a Rangers game and catch up on my sleep."

Teresa sat down across from Jack. She strained to smile and timidly spoke to him. "How's it going this morning?"

He hardly glanced up at her. "Oh, okay."

"Phyllis, if I can help with anything at all..." said Teresa.

"Don't even think of it. Everything's in hand. Julia's going to help me a bit later, and I think I've conned Frank into lending some muscle."

Frank grimaced. "Mother, Julia and I will be visiting some friends this morning. We might be back by mid-afternoon, but I'm not sure. So don't count on us."

Phyllis glared back. "Really, Frank, I need your help." She looked at Teresa, shook her head and said disgustedly, "Kids."

Teresa could see that Phyllis was nervous. She fretted about one thing and then another, she asked Gloria the same question twice, and she forgot that she had already gulped down her glass of orange juice.

"Honey, why don't you settle down? You're even making *me* nervous," said George as he picked the *Morning News* off the serving table. "Well, I'm going upstairs with the paper."

After Frank and Julia left, Phyllis looked at Jack. "Jack, are you all right this morning?"

"I'm fine. Just a bit tired. I guess the week is finally catching up with me."

"Teresa," Phyllis asked, "what's happening with the mystery?"

"Oh, Phyllis, you're too busy to worry about that right now. Let's just say that you don't want your party to end up like Sarah's."

"Huh?"

"You sure you want to hear about this?"

"Of course." Phyllis sat down and tried to focus on Teresa's story about her dream.

"What about the coins?" asked Jack. "Anything happen with the coins?"

Teresa responded, "Uh...no. Nothing happened as far as I know." She thought for a moment. "And we still need to locate that dagger."

"Are you sure there really *is* a dagger?" Jack asked. "I mean, nobody except you...in this day and age, anyway...has actually seen it."

"Oh, there's a dagger. We just have to find it."

"Well, Charles probably has it, dear, and we don't know where Charles is," said Granger.

"Maybe," said Teresa. "How about we go out to Charles's place on the lake to see if we can find it."

"You can try, but I don't think he'll be very cooperative. I'll give you directions," said Phyllis.

Chapter Twenty-Six

"Ugh, it even *smells* moldy out here," said Teresa as she and Granger parked at the small frame house on the edge of the lake. She pulled a handkerchief out of her purse and wiped the perspiration off her forehead.

"Yeah, and listen to those bull frogs. Bet they're glad they live where there's cool water," said Granger. Say, what happened to Jack? I thought he was coming, but he bombed out on us."

"Uh...he said he was tired. I guess he's just going to take some time to rest."

Granger slapped his left arm. "Mosquitoes. They love this water too."

"Charles!" Teresa yelled after opening the screen and pounding on the front door. "Charles! It's Mrs. Walker." She heard no response. "Charles! Please! I know you're inside because your car is out here."

A muffled voice responded, "All right. Just a minute."

Charles opened the door only an inch or two. "What do you want? I don't work at the Runyon place anymore."

"We know, but we want to talk to you."

"I don't have anything to say to you, ma'am."

"Charles, please. We have some questions. We know who you are. We even have a picture of you and your dad." Charles took the old picture when Teresa offered it through the small opening.

"Umm...yeah. That's my dad and me." He chuckled and opened the door a bit more. "I forgot about this picture." He looked at them for a moment. "Okay. You can come in. But I don't know if I'm going to answer your questions."

"Charles, we know you changed your name so that people wouldn't know you're a Bollinger. Why'd you do that? Why didn't you just keep the Bollinger name?" asked Granger after they sat down.

"Can't say."

A frustrated Teresa decided to play a trump card. "You know, we could go to the sheriff and tell him about your masquerade, like how you took the identity of Charles Breck. The law probably wouldn't look very favorably on you for doing that...stealing someone else's social security number and all. But if you answer our questions, we might be persuaded to keep quiet."

"You wouldn't. I've built up a work history and everything using the Breck name. It'd ruin me."

"That's right," responded Teresa. "It *would* ruin you, just like your dad was ruined during the Depression." She wouldn't normally have pulled such an underhanded rabbit out of her hat, but in this case she felt justified.

"Well...."

"Well what?" asked Granger.

"You must understand how I felt. At one time my parents owned that house. I remember living there when I was very young, and it was a wonderful part of my life. But my dad fell on bad times during the thirties, then he went off to war and, well, my mom just couldn't hold it all together. By the time he returned, it was too late. They had to sell out." He sighed. "I was about nine by then. We had to move into...uh...less than desirable quarters. I was never able to go back to the house. That is, until I got a job there."

"Why did you take on this alternate identity?" asked Teresa.

"Oh, it was just too embarrassing. I mean, a Bollinger working in the jobs I had to do...you know." He stopped for a moment and stared blankly as if in a trance. "You'd be surprised how easy it was to take another man's name—kind of scary, really. Nobody ever checked. Nobody ever asked any questions. I guess everybody's just too busy with their own lives, just trying to make a living. I suppose I was able to stay below the radar. I was such a loner, even the people who knew me when I was young ignored me."

"Yeah. Go on," insisted Granger.

"Well, it took a long time before I was able to get back into the house. I never had much hope. But then, well, the Runyons came along, and they had this job, and through what you might call 'connections', they hired me. These last ten years or so have been the best. It was like I owned the place. Mr. and Mrs. Runyon are real nice people too. They've always treated me like...well, family."

"Charles, tell us what you know about Sarah."

Charles bristled. "I can't say anything about that."

"Oh, so you *do* know something. Why can't you tell us?"

"It's private. It's family."

"Yes, but you must know that I've been drawn into it. Just like you, I have a vested interest in what happened to Sarah."

"Yes ma'am, but..."

Granger interjected, "Charles, we didn't *ask* to get involved in this thing. Mrs. Walker and I, well, we were just swept into it. We think Sarah and her mother are...uh...for want of a better term, *communicating* with her. They want the mystery solved, and they won't really be at rest until it is. We didn't volunteer for this, but we're in it nevertheless."

"Yeah, well..."

"Don't you see you'd be helping them, Sarah and her mother, if you help us?" pleaded Teresa.

Charles shook his head and looked down at the floor. "I...I swore I'd never talk to anybody about it, but I see you're, well, almost like family now too."

"More than you might think, Charles," said Teresa.

Charles took a deep breath. "The story that I always heard was that Sarah and this guy Lance...Lance Feldcamp...were going to elope against her mother's wishes the night of a big party. He was a lot older than Sarah, and he was a no-account. He was rich and all, but he was a gambler and *not* a gentleman. You know, that was real important back then. Seems he was well known in New Orleans and Natchez and such places. He was always out for money and a good time. You have to understand how it was in those days. The Bollingers, well, they were at the top of the heap socially. They were aristocrats. If Sarah had married this Feldcamp guy, it would've embarrassed the whole family." He shook his head again. "I remember my grandmother saying, 'It just wouldn'ta been right.' She just kept saying that over and over. 'It just wouldn'ta been right.' I guess she was still trying to be an aristocrat herself. Anyway, Sarah was determined to marry this guy, up to the end anyways."

"What happened? Did they meet that night?" asked Teresa.

"Well, so the story goes. But, right then they had big argument. It seems Sarah had second thoughts about going against her mother's wishes. She told Lance she loved him and wanted to marry him but couldn't."

Teresa's pulse quickened. "So?"

"So, in a fit of rage, Lance killed her with a dagger. Then he sort of disappeared. 'Course, to keep appearances, the family had to cover up how she died. They didn't tell the authorities, didn't tell anybody. They said she was killed in an accident, and it was all just dropped. I guess it was easy to fool everybody, with their position in society and all."

"Do you believe that story, Charles?" asked Teresa.

"I *did*."

"What do you mean *did*?"

"Well…I…"

"Did you find out something that refutes the story you just told us?" Granger asked.

"I can't say."

"Charles, please," pleaded Teresa. "What about the dagger?"

"I don't know *anything* about the dagger."

"But you know about the tunnel, and you know we found a trunk in the basement."

"Yes, yes."

"So you found the dagger."

"No. I didn't find the dagger. I looked for it. I wanted to find it. But I didn't."

"Charles…"

"You have to believe me. I don't know where the dagger is."

"Okay," said Granger, "what about the pages in the diary."

"Pages?"

Teresa was persistent. "Yes, the last three pages of Sarah's diary—the entries for January 7th and 8th and another page after that."

"Oh, that, well…"

"Yeah, that."

"I don't have them."

"What did you do with them?"

"I left them at the house."

"Where?"

"In the basement by the trunk."

Teresa and Granger looked at each other. "Okay, but even if you don't have the pages, you read them, didn't you?" asked Teresa.

"Uh...yeah...of course."

"What did they say, Charles?"

"I can't tell you. I'm drawing the line right there."

"You have to tell us. It's vital."

"No. No way."

"All right. Just tell us this: Did Sarah and Lance meet at the cemetery that night?"

Charles closed his eyes. "Yes, yes they met the night of the party. The diary confirmed that part of the story. I'll tell you that much, but that's it. Now go away and leave me alone. I don't have anything you want now, not the dagger, not the pages from the diary. Just leave, *please*."

Teresa could see that Charles had been stretched to the limit. They would get no more information from him, at least not right now. They thanked him for his help and drove away.

"What do you think was written on those pages?" asked Granger.

"Something devastating, something that shattered all Charles's notions, all his fantasies about his family. He's a broken man, Granger. In a way, he's still that little boy in the picture setting out trees with his dad. You know, he said the Bollingers were at the top of the heap. They had status, and they lost it all. He said his parents never got over their misfortune during the Depression, but I think he never did either. He had some lofty vision of what his family was, but whatever was on those pages was the final blow. Whatever family pride he had left was crushed when he read the diary."

"Hmm...yeah. Crushed. So how will we ever find out what was really on the pages and who has them now?"

Teresa's brain was working overtime. "I'm not sure, but I think I know."

"Jack?"

"Maybe."

"Why wouldn't he tell us he has them?" asked Granger.

Teresa bit her lip because she didn't want to lie to Granger, but she knew she must. "Don't know that either."

"So how will we get them from him?"

"Just be patient, dear, just be patient."

Chapter Twenty-Seven

Jack was getting desperate. Behind the locked door of his bedroom he removed the sheathed dagger from the suitcase and admired it once again. Then he reached back inside the compartment where the dagger had been hidden and pulled out three yellowed sheets of paper filled with faded handwriting. He read the words scribbled across the first two pages.

Sunday, January 7, 1855

I attended the short worship service in the parlor this morning. Robert read from Isaiah. He is so authoritative, so knowledgeable about the Lord's Word, but I still miss Father's reassuring voice. Later, Mother and I worked on our sewing, and I read from Mr. Dickens' book. I passed a note circuitously to Lance, but I made Carrie swear not to say anything to Mother about it. I am secretly putting some things into a valise to take with me when we meet. Only a few more days and we will be off.

Several guests arrived today to stay until the party on Tuesday.

Monday, January 8, 1855

Tomorrow night Lance and I will meet in the cemetery at ten. I know it sounds gruesome, but I think of it as a symbolic burial of my old ways before starting a new life. I love him so. Mother still lectures me about Lance's reputation. I know his behavior is repugnant, but I think I can change him. Robert knows about our plans, and he told me today that he has reservations about Lance. This is a surprise as he has always been supportive in the past. I think he is to talk to Lance tomorrow.

Jack held the last page in his hand and chuckled. He thought perhaps he should burn the wrinkled piece of paper to destroy all evidence of what really happened. After reading it, Jack could understand why Charles left. Perhaps, he thought, he could extract some value from the information.
"Hello."
"Hello, Charles?"
"Yes."
"This is Jack McAlester. You know, at the Runyon house."
"Uh...yes, Mr. McAlester. But I don't work there anymore."
"Oh, I know. I'm calling you on another matter."
"Another matter?"
"Yes. A business matter, so to speak."
"I found some information you might be interested in having, or at least in keeping other people from having."
Charles froze. "What information?"
"I have the pages from the diary, Charles."
"Oh, you found them. So?"
"Well it's pretty damning for the Bollingers."
"Why would I care what happened over a hundred years ago?"
"Because you're a Bollinger."
"So what?"
"So you admit your name's not Breck."
"What do you want, Mr. McAlester?"
"We need to talk. How about meeting in the cemetery tonight, say about ten? Okay?"
"The cemetery?" Charles thought for a moment. "Well, okay. Tonight at ten."
"See you then, Charles."
"Uh...yes. See you then."
Jack turned off his cell phone and smiled. He thought about how much of the money could become his and about how, with such lar-

gess actually in his grasp, he might yet be able to persuade Teresa to abandon Granger. Yes, he must focus on Teresa. After all, he really was running out of time.

******

Teresa and Granger arrived back at the mansion just as the caterer was unloading two long buffet tables from his truck. The lawn in front of the house was a mess. Several delivery vans were lined up near the porch steps, torches were being set up along both sides of the driveway, and a gardener was setting out large earthen pots of blooming plants between the columns.

"Quite a production," said Granger.

"Yeah. I guess Phyllis is going whole hog," responded Teresa.

Just as they were about to enter the house, Teresa stopped and grabbed Granger by the arm.

"Wait," ordered Teresa.

"What is it?"

"I don't know. Something's changed here."

"Huh?" Granger wrinkled his forehead. "You're having another one of those visions, aren't you dear?"

"No. Not a vision. I just think something's going on that we should be afraid of."

"Now what?"

"I can't quite pinpoint what it is, but it's cold...evil."

"*Evil?*"

"Yes." Teresa felt a strong emotion of dread, as if she were about to enter a dark cave. "It's black. It's something that means us harm, Granger."

"One of your ghosts?"

"No, of course not. It's something alive and tangible, and it's in the house now."

"Don't be silly. If it's alive and tangible, we can deal with it." He pulled away from her.

She let go of his arm and stammered, "Okay, let's go in, but be careful."

"Back already?" said Phyllis. She was running helter-skelter, talking with the caterer in one room, the butler or one of his assistants in another, and Gloria in a third. The furniture had been displaced from its usual arrangement to create wide open spaces in the rooms. In the dining room the serving tables were being assembled and covered with crisp white and smaller decorative green linen cloths. The catering crew was manhandling a huge block of ice that would soon become a large sculpture, and Gloria was having a particularly difficult time negotiating with the caterer's staff for space to do her own work.

"Mrs. Runyon, these guys are in my way in the kitchen. I'm going to have to snatch one of them baldheaded."

"Gloria," admonished Phyllis, "they need some space too. And watch out for that man who's doing the sculpture. He looks mean with that ice pick he's waving around."

Gloria's mouth flew open. "Mrs. Runyon, you don't think he's dangerous, do you?"

Phyllis laughed. "No, Gloria. I think you're more of a danger to *him* than he is to you."

"I feel awful just sitting around," said Teresa.

"Don't worry. Everything's going fine. This is the time of maximum mass confusion before any party like this. It's really going well even though it appears to be disorganized." She frowned. "But I wish Frank and Julia would show up. They *could be* helping a little bit."

Teresa and Granger felt like fifth wheels, so they excused themselves and went upstairs. Jack's bedroom door was closed, but the door to the old west bedroom, Sarah's room, was ajar.

"Did you notice the door to Sarah's bedroom was cracked open a bit?" asked Teresa after they closed their door behind them.

"Yeah. So?"

"You know, I've never seen it left open. Phyllis keeps it closed and the AC shut off in there most of the time. Wonder why it's open now?"

"I don't know, dear. Aren't you just being overly suspicious?"

"Maybe. Uh...I think I'll go check it out."

Stifling a yawn, Granger said, "You want me to come with you?"

"No need. I'll be right back."

Teresa shut the bedroom door behind her, walked down the hall and climbed the four steps to the old part of the house. The west bedroom door was still open slightly. She could hear Phyllis and the others downstairs still chattering away about party preparations. That feeling of dread, cold and dark, suddenly reappeared, and she wondered whether its source was in the bedroom. She crept close to the door and listened. Over the background noise from downstairs, she could hear slight movements inside, as if a rat were darting around the room. She waited for a moment and then pushed gently on the door and slowly walked inside.

She jumped. "Oh...uh...Jack. Didn't know it was you. I...I saw the door was ajar, and I heard a noise." She felt uncomfortable and thought she should beat a hasty retreat.

Jack grinned strangely. "That's okay." He moved closer and pushed the door closed. "Come in."

"No...well...I probably should go on down to my room. Granger's waiting for me." She had to have a reason to leave. "And we have an appointment."

"Oh? Well, I have an appointment too, Teresa." Jack talked in a very calm voice, but it was too calm, almost eerily soothing to the ear. Scenes of old Peter Lorre movies flashed through her mind: sinister, wicked, and pernicious.

"You do? Then I should let you go." She started to back away from him and reach for the doorknob.

"Wait," he said. "I want to talk to you."

"I don't think that's such a good idea. Besides, your appointment..."

"Oh, it's not until tonight. It's with someone you might want to see."

"Who's that?"

"Charles. I'm meeting Charles tonight...at ten in the cemetery."

"Charles? Why? At the cemetery? That's kind of late to be in a cemetery, isn't it?" She felt herself shaking, and her back was almost against the door.

"It wasn't too late for Sarah and Lance to meet there." He smiled again, and Teresa felt another chill. "And it's not too late for us, either."

"Now Jack, we've already talked about this."

He took her hand. "Teresa, Charles and I are going to make a deal. I'm going to get a piece of those gold coins. They're worth millions...*millions*. She could see the determination on his face.

She fumbled with the knob behind her, opened the door, and almost ran back to her bedroom. Securely inside the locked door, she felt her legs weaken, and she sat down, breathless and frightened, in the chair next to the desk. Thank goodness Granger couldn't see her because he was in the bathroom. She couldn't believe what was happening. Apparently, after she defeated her demons, they had leaped onto Jack, and now they were eating him alive. She thought for a few minutes about just packing up and leaving right then, before the party. She and Granger could drive off down that winding driveway, pass through the gate and escape. Thoughts of the places they could go raced through her mind. She always loved London: the plays, the castles, Regent Street. Or, Barbados: Now, there's another wonderful refuge: tropical breezes, wide whitewashed verandas, rum-laced fruit drinks and huge gardens of colorful orchids. She looked out the window toward the Balfour water tower and wondered what was going to happen when Jack and Charles met at the cemetery. How did Jack know that Sarah and Lance had met at *ten* at the *cemetery*? *She* knew because of one of her dreams, but she had not revealed those details to anybody. That information must be revealed in the missing diary pages. So, Jack must have them.

She was conflicted. She wanted to run and hide, but on the other hand, she felt obligated to stay to the end. For some time Teresa sat weighing her options. Finally, she mouthed a silent prayer and decided to stick it out. In fact, she knew she had to go to the cemetery at ten as well. That was where the final act would be played out in the story that had begun so long ago.

Chapter Twenty-Eight

"I've been sending emails all over the place this afternoon," said George. "It seems like that's the only way I can get some work done around here." He was drinking coffee at the breakfast table next to the crowded kitchen. Raising a steaming mug in front of Granger, he asked, "Want a cup?"

"That sounds good."

"The pot's on the counter over there. I'm still having trouble with jet lag, so I figure this is just the ticket."

Granger yawned as he sat down and raised the hot cup to his lips. "Pretty wild around here right now." He watched Phyllis run into and out of the kitchen three times within a span of a minute.

George shook his head. "You're right about that. I'd just as soon have stayed in London, but Phyllis more-or-less ordered me home for this party. She's been planning it forever, and in one of my weaker moments I promised I'd be here." He chuckled. "I guess we're all suckers for our wives."

"I guess."

"You grew up in Balfour, didn't you?"

"Yes, but I've lived away for years and years."

"I'm not from Balfour, of course," George drawled.

"So, why did you end up here, of all places?"

"Oh...that...well, let's just say I love the fishing. 'Course, I never have time to do it." George quickly added, "Say, you might know a few of the people coming tonight."

"Oh, I was wondering about that."

George lowered his voice to almost a whisper and looked around to make sure no one else was nearby. "One other thing about tonight: Uh...my kids, Frank and Julia, they talked to me about this mystery thing. I don't know much about it. Sounds really interesting to me, but they thought it'd be best if we...uh...you and your wife and..."

"Jack. Jack McAlester," prompted Granger.

"Uh...yeah, Jack didn't mention anything about it tonight. And I talked to Phyllis."

"Yes, yes. I know. We understand. Nobody will mention it."

"Seems they have some sensibilities, as they say. They think it might reflect badly on the family."

"I understand."

"Now I don't exactly agree with 'em. I think it's a hoot. In fact, those Brits I work with on the other side of the pond called it 'bloody ripping'. You know, they get a lot of flak what with all the ghosts that overpopulate the UK. They were tickled to hear that some Texas good ol' boy had one or two in his *own* house."

Granger chuckled. "Well, I can see why they might like that." He poured another portion of steaming liquid into his cup.

George continued, "Say, who *is* this Jack McAlester anyway? You know him much better than I do, but I confess I've had some trouble getting through to him. Seems like a strange guy."

"Well, I don't know him very well either. We met less than a week ago. Why do you ask?"

"He came downstairs a while ago with a suitcase and said he had to leave. Phyllis was real busy then, out back somewhere. You know how she's been. Anyway, he asked me to thank her for her hospitality, and he drove away in his rent car."

Granger's eyes popped open wide. "Drove away?"

"Yep."

"You mean he packed up and left?"

"Yeah. In fact, I asked Gloria to go upstairs and check his room and, sure enough, he'd cleaned out all his stuff."

"Did he say where he was going?"

"Nope. Just said thanks and good-bye."

"Hmm...I can't believe that. He was...that is, *we* were working on this thing together. I thought we'd built up a good relationship, and he didn't say anything about leaving before morning. He had a flight back to San Francisco tomorrow, but I thought he'd be here through the night. I'll have to ask Teresa about this."

"Beats me," said George. "You know how those Yankees are, though. Sometimes you just can't figure 'em out."

"Yeah." Puzzled, Granger smiled and swallowed another mouthful of coffee.

******

"Carrie, help me here," ordered Sarah as she struggled to pull the small suitcase from its hiding place under her bed. "And ask Peter to come carry it for me."

"Miss Sarah, you sure you know what you're doin'?" asked Carrie.

"Believe me, Carrie, I know. I'm a grown woman...well, mostly grown anyway. I can do whatever I want."

"But your mother is downstairs wonderin' where you are. You oughta go back down to the party."

"Carrie, call Peter. Now that's an order."

Carrie opened the bedroom door to leave just as Robert was walking up.

"Sarah, where are you going?" asked Robert.

"To meet Lance. We're eloping. You know." Sarah was primping in front of the mirror.

"I don't know about all this. I...I've come around to Mother's point of view. At least wait for a while to make sure."

Sarah turned and frowned at him. "Now, Robert. You're going back on your word. You've always supported me in my relationship with Lance. Why this change of mind?"

"Well, Lance *is* a gambler and a scurrilous rogue. He wouldn't make a good husband for you. There are too many others closer to your age, with breeding and the proper education...."

She interrupted, "Robert! Don't talk like that. You sound just like Mother. Don't you see that I love Lance, and nothing you or Mother could say will change that? I really don't care *what* his history's been. He's going to start a new life with me after we're married."

"But, Sarah, he's not going to change. You might think he will, but it won't happen. I know men like him. They're all the same. I've seen them rolling dice in the gambling houses in Natchez and hanging around the...uh...bordellos in New Orleans."

"You know about bordellos? Well, I declare, Robert." Sarah picked up a small bottle of perfume. "Now you just stop talking about Lance."

"Sarah, I'm going with you to meet Lance tonight. I'm going to try to talk some sense into him even if I can't get *you* to listen to me."

"But, Robert." Tears streamed down her face.

"No buts. Where are you meeting him?"

"Robert, I..."

"*Where?*"

"In the cemetery at ten."

He pulled out his watch. "Hmm...only about an hour from now. I'll meet you there. I just have to get something to take with me." He opened the door and stormed out.

******

"Granger, I have to talk to you," said Teresa.

"I want to talk to you too. Just give me a minute."

"Now, Granger, please!" She grasped his forearm and pulled.

He could see she was determined. "George, would you excuse me?"

"Sure," said George as a knowing grin grew across his face. "Guess you're getting one of those orders from *your* wife this time."

"Yeah, right."

Teresa led Granger to the relatively quiet and private back portion of the entry foyer near the entrance to the basement stairs. She whispered, "Granger, I had another revelation. I know what happened that night, the night of Sarah's party."

"Yeah, well, I have some hot information too."

"Huh?"

"You won't believe this, but Jack left."

"Left? You mean *gone?*" she said out loud.

"He packed his bag, thanked Phyllis for having him here, and drove away."

"He won't be back?"

"I guess not. Doesn't that beat all?"

"Yeah." Teresa tried to absorb this news that only flooded her mind with more questions.

"Okay, dear, what did your 'revelation' tell you?" Granger asked.

Teresa refocused. "Well, Sarah and Lance arranged to meet at ten in the cemetery. Robert came to Sarah's room and told her he now agreed with Vivian and opposed her relationship with Lance. And, get this: Robert told Sarah he was going to be at the cemetery too."

"So you think all three of them were there at ten."

"That was the plan."

"Hmm. That opens up more possibilities."

"It sure does. And, Granger, there's another thing."

"What *else* could there be?"

"Uh...Jack..."

"Yeah. Jack what?" Granger suddenly felt uneasy.

"Jack's meeting Charles at the cemetery tonight at ten."

Teresa could see that Granger was stunned. "Jack's meeting Charles? How do you know, and why would he do that anyway?"

Teresa hesitated. She wanted desperately to reveal everything to him. "Let's just say I have insight based on personal experience. And, as far as why, well..."

"Yeah?"

"Well, I think Jack's trying to extort money from Charles."

"Money from Charles? He's not a rich man."

"But he might be rich once the Double Eagles are sold....that is, if he reveals that he's a direct Bollinger heir. And remember, they could be worth several million dollars."

"Hmm. So why would they be meeting at the cemetery, of all places."

"Warped sense of history I guess. I don't really know." She grabbed Granger's arm again and said firmly, "One thing I *do* know, dear, is that *we* have to be there tonight as well."

"*We* do? Why? Let's just stay out of it. I have *no* desire to be wandering around that cemetery, or *any* cemetery, at ten o'clock at night. The mere thought of it gives me the willies."

Teresa glared at him. "Don't you *understand*? This is the endgame. It's where we're going to find out what really happened to Sarah, and I *have* to be there. Don't you see?" Teresa saw the perplexed look on Granger's face. No amount of education could have prepared him for this situation. She knew that the analytical part of his brain was flashing warnings to him: bells and whistles and blaring sirens. Teresa's composure suddenly changed and her hand slipped into his. Smiling, she said, "This time think with your heart, dear, not your head."

When he looked into her determined eyes, she could see his resistance crumbling. Softly he replied, "Yes. I see. We'll be there tonight too."

Chapter Twenty-Nine

"*Finally*," exclaimed Phyllis as Frank and Julia entered through the front door.

Frank waved his arm toward the front yard. "Quite a mess out there," he said.

"Just *where* have you two been?" demanded Phyllis.

"We told you, Mom. We went to see a few friends over at the old diner. You know: Susie, Hank and Bill," said Julia. "By the way, isn't Susie coming tonight?"

"I think so, but that's not the point." In no mood to consult the official guest list, Phyllis ordered, "Come on. Help Gloria and me with the candles." She handed each of them a crystal candelabra to place on one of the tables in the parlor.

Despite Phyllis's protestations, Teresa and Granger busied themselves with minor decorating duties. In the late afternoon light, Chris lit the torches lining the driveway and made last minute checks of all the decorations. The caterers placed the block of ice, miraculously transformed into a flying eagle, in the middle of the large table in the dining room and stationed huge platters of finger food on other smaller ones around the living area. Gloria rubbed her arms to keep warm because the air conditioning had been cranked down to keep the sculpture as cool as possible. A wine and liquor bar was set up at one end of the dining room. The large area rug in the parlor was mostly void of furniture now, as the couches and chairs were clustered in small conversation areas on the perimeter of the room. Finally, everyone disappeared upstairs to get dressed.

"Looks really nice," said Teresa as she and Granger dressed in their bedroom.

"Yeah, fancy," replied Granger. He was straining to create a bow in the disobedient tie around his neck.

Teresa saw his distress. "Here, let me help you."

While she was working on the tie, Granger inquired, "I'm not sure I want to ask, but I guess I have to. What exactly are you proposing to do about the…uh…meeting tonight?"

"Well, I suppose we just enjoy the party—that is, until about nine thirty. Then we discreetly disappear, and we walk to the cemetery. You know, down the old path from the back of the house."

"Walk? I thought we'd drive. Why couldn't we could just sit in the car and see what happens?"

As she admired the knot she had created, Teresa frowned and shook her head. "Don't be silly. We couldn't *drive*. Someone, like Jack or Charles, would see us coming. We have to sneak up on them to find out what's going on."

"Uh…but are you sure you really want to *walk*?"

"It's the only way."

Teresa flashed a quick grin at him and went into the bathroom to brush her hair.

"One other thing: what did you say to Phyllis about Jack?" yelled Granger.

"Nothing really. She was too busy to worry about it."

"Hmm. Yeah. Guess she had other things on her mind."

******

In the bedroom downstairs, George and Phyllis were also dressing for the party.

"Honey, I have to tell you something. I know it's not a *good* time, but, unfortunately, this is the *only* time we'll have," said George.

"What's that?"

"I talked to Charles this afternoon."

"Charles? Why on earth did you talk to Charles? You shouldn't be making contact with him right now, not with…you know…our guests here. Someone might suspect something."

"Don't you think I'm aware of that? I had to find out why he left."

"Well, did you?"

"Yes. Unfortunately."

Phyllis stopped what she was doing. "So, why did he leave?"

"He read the last few pages of the diary."

"And?"

"That last page: it was written after Sarah was killed."

"Yes, so?" Phyllis had picked up a strand of pearls and was nervously rolling it in her fingers.

"Well, things didn't go exactly as we all thought. And you know how important the Bollinger heritage has always been to Charles."

"Yes."

"He just couldn't handle it. The information on that piece of paper sort of destroyed whatever illusions he had left. He had to get away...escape, if you know what I mean." George heaved a long sigh. "He should've shredded those pages, especially that last one. So now we have a big problem."

"Problem?"

"Jack found and read them too."

"Jack? Jack McAlester?"

"Yeah. Now he's trying to make some kind of deal about the coins with Charles. In fact, they're meeting tonight...at the cemetery."

"But, in order to lay claim to any of the coins, Charles would have to admit he falsified his identity. Isn't that some sort of crime?"

"Well, I guess it would be up to him whether he'd rather continue with his ruse or possibly get a cut of a large sum of money."

Phyllis's eyes widened. "And why are they meeting at the *cemetery*?"

"I don't know the answer to that one. And, dear, this is the part I particularly didn't want to tell you: I'm going with him."

"George, *no*! It's too dangerous. Let Charles handle his own problems."

"But, honey, they're sort of mine too. Don't you see?"

"Well...*no*...I mean, *yes*. I suppose. But, it's too risky. Why don't you just call the sheriff?"

"I was hoping this could be handled without more embarrassment for Charles, or the rest of us, for that matter. He could even end up in prison."

She reached around his neck, pulled his face to hers and kissed him.

"George, I'm so frightened. Please be careful. Remember I need you more than Charles does."

"Yes, dear, and I need you too."

******

"Dotty!" cried Granger as he stood at the entrance to the parlor.

"Why, Granger Walker, it's been a *very* long time," replied Dotty. As she offered her hand and a perfunctory cheek kiss, her smile disappeared. "This is my husband Harold. Harold, this is an old high school classmate of mine, Granger Walker. He was the brain of the class. I was just the mouth." She burst into her trademark broad, deep laugh.

As he shook hands with the overweight bald man in front of him, Granger thought how true that statement was. He grinned and protested, "Now, Dotty. You know I enjoyed every minute of our classes together."

"Yeah," she joked, "*in spite of* me and all my friends."

Granger could see that Dotty's personality, as well as her laugh, hadn't changed at all. Seeing an old familiar face unexpectedly comforted him. He had known her since elementary school, and, though almost forty years had passed since they last saw each other, they fell immediately into a warm conversation. Ignoring Harold, Dotty launched into an amazing monologue detailing her life since high school—marriage, kids and, recently, grandchildren.

"You have kids?" she asked.

Uneasily, Granger answered, "Uh...no. Teresa and I travel and keep up our house and garden now. Footloose and fancy free, as they say."

"Must be nice."

"Uh...yeah, nice. Say, let me get you a drink."

"Sure. Thanks. I'll be over on the couch."

"Teresa," said Granger when he saw her at the bar. "Dotty." He pointed toward the couch in the corner.

"Dotty?"

"Yeah. That's her over there. You know, one of 'The Three'."

"Oh. So, *that's* her? Well, I have to meet this one."

"Dotty, this is my wife Teresa," said Granger as he handed her the drink. "I got you a rum and coke. I seem to recall you had a weakness for them at one time."

"Why, Granger, you're right. I can't believe you remembered such a little thing like that." Dotty took the drink and turned to Teresa. "It's so good to meet you." Immediately she grinned at Granger.

"Why, Granger, you lucky dog. How in the world did such a brain capture such a beauty?"

Both Granger and Teresa laughed.

"I'm not sure about the beauty part," said Teresa. "I'm way past the beauty stage, I'm afraid."

The time passed quickly as Granger chatted with Dotty and several other Balfour natives he had known at one time or another. As the hours passed, Granger reestablished his long-broken friendships with Dotty and the other classmates who were there. The evening was a metamorphosis for him. Old adolescent connections were renewed and miraculously transformed into new adult relationships. He began to recognize that any animosities or lingering youthful discomforts had disappeared into the mists of the past and that they were now merely impotent memories that didn't matter anymore.

"Teresa," he said when they were alone later, "you know, I'm starting to see that some things I thought were so important really *aren't* anymore."

"What?"

"Well, everyone is so friendly me tonight. I mean, it's like we're really *friends*."

"Of course, dear. That's what I've been telling you. Anything that happened back then is...well...ancient history...gone...over. Now only *you* have to let it go. They obviously did, a long time ago. Despite any differences, the fact is that you all have shared a lot of experiences."

"Yes. You're right, I see that now."

"Welcome to the twenty-first century, honey."

******

About nine o'clock, Granger ran into George in the dining room.

"Great party," said Granger.

"You know, surprisingly, I'm enjoying it too." He sipped at his drink and then, with a more serious demeanor, he leaned closer to Granger. "Say, I want to give you something I think you might need tonight."

Granger's eyes widened. "Oh? What's that?"

"Come with me," he said as he motioned for Granger to follow him out of the room.

"Now close the door behind you," ordered George after they entered the master bedroom. He went straight to a small end table, pulled a key out of his pocket and unlocked the top drawer. "Here. I think you should have this." He pulled out a small snub-nosed revolver, opened the chamber, and then closed it. "Yeah. It's loaded." Then he handed it to Granger.

Taken aback, Granger stammered, "George, why do you think I need to have *this* thing?"

"Oh, I don't know. Let's just say a little bird told me you might need it tonight."

"That little bird must be clairvoyant."

George smiled knowingly. "Just tell Teresa she isn't the only one who knows what's going on around here."

Granger slipped it into the inside pocket of his jacket and grinned. "For what it's worth, thanks."

******

At nine thirty, Teresa found Granger still talking to Dotty and a small group of other people in the parlor. She could tell that he was nervous because he seemed to be laughing at almost any old high school war story anyone was telling.

"Please excuse us," she said. "Come, dear, we have to go." She tugged on his arm.

"You ready?" she asked as they exited the house via the chaotic kitchen onto the back porch.

"Not really. Are you *sure* you want to do this?"

"Surer than ever. This is the only way both Sarah and I can be free. We have to see it through to the end."

Making certain no one saw them leave, they stepped off the porch, passed the old smokehouse and started walking down the stone pathway toward the cemetery. The night was warm and still and clear. Only the sounds of night creatures disturbed the dark solitude. Overruling his objections, Teresa wouldn't let Granger use a small flashlight he'd crammed into his trouser pocket just before they left the house.

"Now, don't talk once we get close," Teresa instructed. "Someone might hear us. We'll hide behind the big granite monument. You know the one."

"Okay, but I still don't understand exactly what we're going to do."

"We're going to listen and let nature take its course."

"Huh?"

"Shhh! We're close now."

By the dim light of the quarter moon, they made their way through the gate and weaved between the headstones to a huge monument, on higher ground than the others, near the middle of the sea of graves. From there, they could look out across the whole cemetery. Row upon row of markers covered the several acres before them. Teresa looked up at the diamond-like stars, millions of them, twinkling overhead. She thought how here, in this one scene, the infinite and the finite were juxtaposed: the unfathomable, immutable stars and the worldly, mortal shells of hundreds of souls.

Chapter Thirty

In the pitch-black, frigid darkness, the carriage arrived at the edge of the cemetery with a driver wrapped tightly in his coat and muffler.

"Stop here," ordered Lance as he thrust his head out the window. Dressed in buckskin pants and boots and gloves, a red vest over a white shirt, and along coat, Lance certainly looked the dashing suitor. "We'll wait here until the lady comes."

Soon, two figures appeared along the stone pathway from the house.

"We shouldn't be here, Miss Sarah. It ain't right to disturb a cemetery at night. The spirits might not like it."

"Peter, don't be foolish. There's nothing to be scared of out here. Everybody's dead."

Peter held his torch higher and tightened his grip on the suitcase. "I know. That's what makes me afraid."

"Oh, just hurry."

As they reached the carriage, they looked back to see another torch moving along the path toward them. Sarah embraced Lance and gasped, "Who's that? Shouldn't we go?"

Lance calmly replied, "No. I know who it is. It's Robert. He said he was going to meet me this evening."

Sarah became even more frantic. "Let's just leave, Lance. We can get into the carriage and be away before he gets here."

"No, my dear. I won't be a coward in front of you." He took off his gloves and slapped them against his thigh. Soon the distant figure approached them. With Sarah clinging to him, Lance said, "Robert. How good of you to come see us off. And on such a cold night too." He surveyed the starry sky. "Could freeze tonight."

"Sarah, you must come back to the house with me," ordered Robert, his breath forming clouds of vapor in front of his face.

"No. I'm going with Lance as we planned."

"Mother and I think it would be best for you to wait a season or two to get married."

Sarah was indignant now. "I really don't care what you *or* Mother thinks. I'm leaving tonight with Lance! We're going to New Orleans to be married and then on to San Francisco."

"Sarah, you can't..."

"Mr. Bollinger, sir," Lance interrupted. "Sarah is old enough to make her own decisions. If she wants to leave with me tonight, then that's what she's going to do."

"I'm still the squire of this family, sir, and I have only *her* and my family's best interests in mind."

"Oh yes," retorted Lance, "you have the family's best interest in mind. That *is* true if by the *family* you mean *you yourself*."

"Not at all, sir."

Lance calmed a bit. "Listen, Robert. We have an agreement. I have…uh…given you ample…uh…consideration. Right?"

Sarah broke in, "Consideration? What do you mean?"

"Nothing, my dear. Nothing."

Robert saw his chance. "Yes, Sarah. You didn't know about this, but your dear Lance here has *paid* for you, just as he would a French whore on some back alley in New Orleans."

"Paid? Paid what?" Sarah implored as her eyes widened.

"Money, my dear sister. Money and lots of it," said Robert.

"Is this *true*, Lance?" she demanded. She turned toward Lance and pulled away from him.

"Well…"

"Oh, and he gave me something else as well. Something personal," said Robert. He pulled the sheathed dagger from inside his coat. "*See.*" He removed the dagger from its scabbard and flashed it around in the light of the torches.

Peter, who had been watching from a short distance, saw the dagger and ran off down the stone path back toward the house.

"Lance!" cried Sarah.

"Yes. I gave Robert some money. It's a loan, my dear. Since I'm going to be in the family, why shouldn't I contribute to the family cause? And, as for the dagger, well it's merely a gift. I saw it in a New Orleans shop and immediately thought of Robert. It was such a fine specimen, made by some one of the best craftsmen in Spain. What's so wrong about giving my future brother-in-law a small gift?"

"Well, Robert, if the money is a loan and the knife just a gift..." said Sarah more calmly.

Robert's anger welled up. "You're a rogue, Mr. Feldcamp, a rogue and a low scoundrel not fit to eat from the slave table."

Lance bristled and pushed Sarah away. "Take that comment back!"

"I will not!"

"Then I must defend my honor."

Lance pulled a small gun out of his coat and raised it over his head. Instantly, Sarah threw herself onto Lance and shrieked, "No!"

By that time, Robert had lifted the dagger and was thrusting at Lance's chest. His arm came down, and the dagger sank deep into Sarah's neck. Crazed, Robert stabbed again and again until she lay lifeless on the cold ground. Covered with Sarah's blood, Lance stared down at her body and up at Robert.

"What have you wrought? It's the devil you'll pay for this," said Lance.

Robert's eyes seemed to turn fiery red. "No. You're the real devil here. If you don't leave, you'll be hanging from a tall oak tree by morning." Lance took a step backward. "I'm going to tell them *you* did it, Mr. Feldcamp. You can stay and take your chances or just leave in that carriage right now. Take your pick. But, if you stay, consider this question: Who do you think everyone around here is going to believe—the respected Bollinger heir or some disreputable rogue from California?"

Lance thought for a minute, sighed and then relented, "All right. I'll go. But what about the carriage driver? He has eyes and ears."

Robert walked over to the carriage while pulling some coins out of his pocket. As he handed them to the driver, he said, "Here's ample payment for your silence. I'd recommend you get lost as well and consider this payment in full for your eternal discretion. You'll rue the day I see you again in these parts."

The driver took the money and moved as far as he could away from Robert and the dagger. While still clutching the knife limply in his right hand, Robert watched as Lance climbed into the carriage and it pulled away into the inky darkness.

A PEACE IN TIME

******

Teresa and Granger waited in the eerie stillness for what seemed like hours. Teresa knew now what had really happened to Sarah during those fateful few minutes so many years ago. She closed her eyes and mouthed a silent prayer.

Impatiently, Granger poked Teresa's arm and pointed at the face of his watch. It was almost ten fifteen. He felt the bulge of the gun in his pocket and closed his eyes. When he opened them, a set of headlights flashed across his face as a car turned into the parking area. Soon a man entered the cemetery through the main gate. Almost simultaneously, he saw the beam of a flashlight probing the darkness along the stone pathway, and he could barely perceive the outline of two figures approaching. As Granger and Teresa hunkered down, the three men met and began talking. Because it was difficult to hear, they moved as close as they dared to the conversation and sidled up to another large marker, but they still could hardly make out the conversation.

Two of the men were clearly Jack and Charles, but the other was cloaked in darkness. Charles directed the beam from his flashlight onto Jack's hand as Jack pointed to something he held in his right palm. They appeared to be arguing. The men turned slightly, and now they could hear.

"The coins. The Double Eagles in the basement," said Jack. "They're ours for the taking and they're worth millions."

Charles shook his head. "But I don't want the money. It's tainted. It's blood money. I know 'cause Robert confessed what he did in the last entry in the diary. Guess he felt remorse and had to get it off his chest. You've read it too."

"Yes, yes. I've read it. But what does that have to do with us? All you have to do is prove you're the last surviving Bollinger heir who lived in the house. You might get *all* the money."

"Yes, but I don't want to reveal I'm a Bollinger. I'm now Charles Breck, not Charles Bollinger. As far as I'm concerned, Charles Bollinger died a long time ago, and I'm *not* a Bollinger. Besides, I'm *not* the last surviving heir anyway."

Even in the darkness, they could tell that Jack was shocked by Charles's revelation.

After a moment of silence, Jack said, "Not the last heir? So, who...?"

"*I* am, Jack," said the other figure. "I'm also a Bollinger."

Teresa's mouth fell open as she recognized the voice. It was George.

She could see that Jack was confused, and he suddenly began to plead. "But, Charles, don't you see. We could have it all. With my help, we could sell the coins."

"No. No. It's over," said Charles. "The Bollingers weren't the honorable family I thought they were. Their fortune, their station...it was all a farce. Robert lied about Sarah's death, and I want no part of it."

"You fool!" Jack screamed. From his coat he pulled out the dagger, lifted it over his head, and thrust downward. George tried to stop him but Jack eluded his reach.

Seeing the dagger, Granger reached into his coat and pulled out the revolver George had given him. Teresa, her eyes transfixed on the struggle, didn't notice. Granger stood up and aimed his gun toward the two men who were now rolling on the ground, but he didn't know what to do. The darkness made it difficult enough to hit a target, and first one and then the other was in the line of fire. Suddenly, one of them let out a gasp and dropped lifelessly onto the grass.

Teresa screamed and turned. "Granger!" she cried as she saw the barrel of gun glisten in the beam of the flashlight she had hurriedly turned on.

The man left standing held the dagger in his right hand, looked at it with unseeing eyes, and dropped it onto the ground next to the bleeding form below him. Quickly Teresa turned the flashlight onto the face of Charles standing over Jack's body and George looking on nearby.

"Charles!" cried Granger with the gun in his hand. "Don't move."

"I...I didn't mean it. He came at me with the knife," protested Charles.

Teresa and Granger walked slowly from their hiding place, and Granger checked Jack to confirm that he was dead.

"Yes," said Teresa to Charles, "we saw what happened. It was self-defense."

"That guy was crazy," said George. "He was out of touch with reality."

Charles knelt down next to Jack's body and looked at it with tears streaming down his cheeks. "I'm sorry. I'm sorry. I didn't mean to do it."

Teresa repeated, "Charles, we know. We saw." Then, after a pause, she said calmly, "At least the *right* person died this time." She reached into her pocket and pulled out her cell phone. "I'll call the sheriff."

******

The night was a blur of sirens, flashing lights and questions from the authorities. Teresa and Granger didn't retire until well after two o'clock, and they slept uneasily until the first rays of morning light filtered in through the curtains. Teresa stood at the open window, inhaled the warm air, and surveyed the fading darkness. As she listened to the songs of the early-rising birds, Granger walked up to her from behind, wrapped his arms around her and placed his face against her cheek.

"Penny for your thoughts," he said.

"My thoughts aren't worth a penny any more," she replied with a slight chuckle.

"Somehow I don't believe that." Then, after a long silence, "Well, is it over, dear?"

"Yes, it's over."

"George's explanations last night helped me understand a lot of the story," said Granger.

"Yeah. It was interesting. I always wondered what happened to Robert and Vivian. Now we know that Robert was killed in the War and that Vivian moved away to New Orleans and left the house with a cousin. Guess she just couldn't bear living here after both Sarah and Robert were gone."

"I suppose."

"She was a broken soul, Granger, but maybe now she and Sarah are *both* at peace."

"I hope so. But, why didn't Robert use any of the money?"

"I guess the guilt got to him. He just couldn't bring himself to use it, and he couldn't reveal how he got it. So, he just stashed it away. And, since nobody else knew where it was hidden, all trace of it was lost."

Granger squeezed her more tightly and asked, "So what did you learn from it all?"

"I learned that in time all deeds, both good and bad, are recognized...that even though the scales may get out of balance for a while, eventually everything evens out. To every thing there is a season...you know."

"Yeah, I know," he said. "And *I* learned that that applies to our lives too."

"I think Sarah and her mother are happy now, and the horrible mistake that Robert made has finally been avenged."

"Are the Bollinger's vindicated?" he asked.

"I don't know about that. All I know is they can all rest more soundly. They have no need to roam these rooms, no reason to cry."

Just then a bug flew up to the window and latched onto the screen.

"Look, Granger," said Teresa.

Granger laughed. "It's a lightning bug. How strange."

"No. Not strange...providential."

Epilogue

Within a month after Jack's death, Charles Breck was cleared of any wrongdoing. He returned to gainful employment and became actively involved in the community with the support of both the Runyons and the Walkers.

Over the following months, Phyllis and George finally cleaned out the contents of the basement. The many artifacts, including the contents of Sarah's trunk and some of the Double Eagles, were donated for display in the museum at the old courthouse. The remaining coins were sold at auction, and the proceeds were used to renovate the museum and to build the new Bollinger Memorial Wing, of which Sarah and her mother would be most proud. Neither Sarah nor Vivian was ever seen again in the mansion, and Granger finally finished the book he had always wanted to write.

Milton Keynes UK
Ingram Content Group UK Ltd.
UKHW030021180324
439604UK00001B/191